Betrayal of a Thug

Lock Down Publications and Ca$h
Presents
Betrayal of a Thug
A Novel by *Fre$h*

Lock Down Publications
Po Box 944
Stockbridge, Ga 30281

Visit our website @
www.lockdownpublications.com

Copyright 2022 by Fre$h
Betrayal of a Thug

First Edition March 2022
Printed in the United States of America

Lock Down Publications
Like our page on Facebook: Lock Down Publications @
www.facebook.com/lockdownpublications.ldp
Book interior design by: **Shawn Walker**
Edited by: **Kiera Northington**

Stay Connected with Us!

Text **LOCKDOWN** to 22828 to stay up-to-date with new releases, sneak peaks, contests and more…
Thank you.

Submission Guideline.

Submit the first three chapters of your completed manuscript to ldpsubmissions@gmail.com, subject line: Your book's title. The manuscript must be in a .doc file and sent as an attachment. Document should be in Times New Roman, double spaced and in size 12 font. Also, provide your synopsis and full contact information. If sending multiple submissions, they must each be in a separate email.

Have a story but no way to send it electronically? You can still submit to LDP/Ca$h Presents. Send in the first three chapters, written or typed, of your completed manuscript to:

LDP: Submissions Dept
Po Box 944
Stockbridge, Ga 30281

DO NOT send original manuscript. Must be a duplicate.

Provide your synopsis and a cover letter containing your full contact information.

Thanks for considering LDP and Ca$h Presents.

Fre$h

Chapter One

It was drizzling outside, and the raindrops only made the candy paint on the 325i BMW gleam more. Yay, which is what the hood called him, was wishing he had stopped procrastinating and paid off the DMV debt he owed. He hated having others drive him around, because the eyes told as much as the lips did. His government name was Seemiyun Baxter, but because of his profession he was only known as Yay.

Tonight, he was supposed to link up with his boy and childhood friend, Han. Han was Chinese and born in Compton, but he moved to North Carolina. His father and drug lord, Han Che, felt he was getting into mischief. Since Han wanted to put in work, Han Che put him to work in the Chinese cartel. He didn't want that life for Han, but Han was too much like his father. Han's mother died over a drug war, a burden Han Che still carried with him, blaming the life he leads. His crew killed everything moving, and Han Che was now invisible somewhere in Virginia. Therefore, he crowned Han his successor and watched Han rule with an iron fist.

As the raindrops fell, Yay glanced at Milk Marie, the new chick he had been bugging on for seven months now. Yay was six-three and two hundred fifty pounds, but he never felt he was a big guy. He moved with the grace of a cheetah, as if the weight wasn't an issue. Brown-skinned with long dreads, he preferred red bones or light skinned chicks. He liked chicks with the big ghetto booty like Nicki Minaj. So how in the hell did he end up with this snow bunny? That's what the hood called white chicks that only mess with black guys.

She liked the hood life, even though she tried to act green to it. He always saw her, but never really paid her any mind. He judged no one, knew she'd been around, but who hadn't? She would always be walking or in a car with some goofy white chicks drinking. She always stood out to him for some reason, but he shook it off.

Then one day, he was bonding one of his boys out on a charge as a favor to Han, and he saw Milk Marie being brought in. She looked extremely stressed, lost, and frustrated. He found out she was chilling with some dude, and she wasn't coming off no pussy. So, the dude left her on the highway with a bottle of vodka. She was pissed off and drinking, walking down the highway and cars were blowing at her as she staggered, trying to walk. Po-Po came through, and the rest was history. His bondsman got her out, and they were honestly cool before any sexual shit popped off. Seven months later, they were still cool.

"Yo, where this Jet Li looking nigga at, bruh? I'm trying to make moves," Polo said from the back seat of the BMW.

Polo and I did a little bid years back. We were pretty cool while in prison. I had a little hustle with the weed, and he had a female C.O. feeling him. We connected, but once we got out, we lost touch. I moved to Elizabeth City, only a few miles from the Virginia line. I was in the hood one day making a play. The nigga pulled up on me asking directions.

"Yo my dude, do you know how to get to the mall?" Polo asked in a Jimmy truck. I had my Gucci shades on, with my dreads in a ponytail with my Cardi hat pulled low, it's obvious he didn't recognize me. So, once I realized who he was, I messed with his head.

"Yo, playa, I don't know you. So, before shit get ugly, you may want to keep it pushing," I said, gripping the butt of the Glock at my waistline.

"Wait. Yo dude, I'm far from pussy. You got a winner, maybe…" he said, staring at me hard. "We will see each other again." Polo started to drive off.

I lifted my shades off my face. "Fool, maybe we already met," I said, smirking my gold grill.

"Yay? Yo, Yay, that's you, nigga?" Polo hopped out, tucking the 9 in his pants and covered his shirt over the butt of the gun.

"Oh word, are you trying to pop me, nigga?" I asked, backing up playfully.

"Naw playa, I not too long got out, better caught with it than without it." We dapped each other and it's been on ever since.

"Bruh, chill, it's not even nine o'clock yet. Besides, it's a pick-up and go, feel me? So relax, I got you on yours," I said impatiently. I never, ever told Polo how much I would get from Han. Not that I didn't trust Polo. Han and Polo had a silent tension between them. One time I had to stop them from fighting in the mall. "Yo, all you wear is Polo. You let one designer define you, playa," Han said playfully in the mall, wearing his signature all-black Armani suit with a gray tie. I looked at Han like, *please don't start*.

"Fool, at least I don't look like Jet Li. Shit… for all I know, you killed Aaliyah, *Romeo Must Die*-looking nigga," Polo said in the middle of Foot Locker. They both started at each other and even the manager, some young white kid said, "Excuse me, sir, is everything alright?"

Han broke the stare, looked at me, wiped some imaginary lint off his Armani suit, adjusted his shades, gave me our signature shoulder bump and walked out. I came out of my thoughts, about to tell Polo when Han pulled up, when the all-black Benz headlights were already pulling up, stopping my words.

We were meeting in a spot called Moyock, between VA and Elizabeth City. We were parked in a closed down flea mall's lot, shut down long ago. It was a good spot, never really any traffic. Then I heard metal on metal behind me as Han's lights turned off.

I've heard that sound a thousand times. It's a chip being fixed in place of a gun. Sometimes I swear he would be showing off for Milk Marie, who was nodding her head to a Nicki Minaj song. "Yo man, what I'd tell you about messing with that ugly ass nine while you sitting behind me? I'm not tripping, because I'm strapped to distract, but this isn't an out-of-town plug on a drought, it's Han," I said, never looking behind me but in the rearview mirror.

"My bad, dang. But, as Suge Knight said to Eazy-E, 'You never know what you need until you need it.' Plus, I may need another gun. This one been acting funny, so it's been a habit to check it. I just haven't gotten around to getting another one."

I paid it no mind, then I asked Milk Marie if she was okay as she stood there looking like a five-one version of perfection. She was killing the Prada dress, with her head still bobbing to Nicki's rapping.

She grinned at me and said, "Go do your thang, baby, because I'm hungry." I slapped her thigh. She swung at me playfully as I got out of the car, wearing an all-black Jordan jogging suit, with my hoodie still on.

As Han was walking towards me, I noticed him nodding at Polo. I looked back in time to see Polo nod back. I gave him the one-clap handshake and our signature shoulder bump.

"Yo, when you two knuckleheads start becoming civil to each other? Maybe that's why it's drizzling out here." I laughed at my own joke, watching Han push a button on his keychain as the trunk popped up. It was dark, but I could see well enough. The way we were parked, cars would drive by and never notice us. This is why we never bought colorful cars, like most hustlers. Drawing attention was the enemy of our profession. Han pulled two big duffel bags out the trunk, but I was only expecting one.

"Damn, is it Christmas? I thought only one..." but before I could finish my sentence, three figures came out of the dark, like out of nowhere. All three had guns aimed at me, Han and my BMW.

"Yo," I spoke up in a confident tone. "Playboy, do you realize who you tryin to rob?" I said, my hand already on the Desert Eagle. I took a quick glance back at the car. "What the fuck is going on?" I thought.

Soon as I turned to face the three robbers, all hell broke loose.

BOOM-BOOM-BOOM

Shots rang out from behind my BMW. I realized Polo had slipped out of the car and took cover behind the BMW. With no hesitation, I whipped out and let my Desert Eagle speak, jumping in my hand like a cannon with every pull of the trigger.

BOOM-BOOM-BOOM

A spray of bullets came at us like the rain that was no longer a drizzle. *Sound like they had Uzi's,* which they did. I was hit and fell back. I heard Milk Marie scream as she ducked in the car seat. I was trying to get up as they were running off with the two duffel bags. One of the guys turned on Han and shot him point-blank range four times, with a handgun.

I could see his chest jumping. I yelled, "No Han! Han!" Still on the ground, I leaned on my left arm and emptied my gun.

BOOM-BOOM-BOOM

"Han! Han!" I yelled. I saw the robber stumble, so I must have hit him. I would have laughed if I wasn't in so much pain. as I saw the robber stagger off, holding his right ass cheek. Then all three vanished.

I could hear Polo hissing, "Yo, come on, man. Han... Han's gone. Let's go." I could hear sirens in the distance, but I ignored Polo, and slid all the way to Han's Benz, where he lay. I held him in my arms and leaned against the Benz. My right shoulder was on fire, and I was drenched from the rain. I just held Han, trying to talk to him as if he could hear me.

"I'm here, homie. I'm here," I said through watery eyes. "Yo Han, what just happened, bruh? Stay with me." But he wasn't moving. I looked up with blurry eyes. I was passing out, yet I could hear Milk Marie beside me. She must have gotten out the car when the coast was clear.

"Hang on, Yay, baby. Hang on." Her voice seemed miles away.

Chapter Two

On a Need-to-Know Basis...

I was floating, and I could see the three dudes masked up. Han was being shot. I was shooting before I blacked out, but there was something—something I was trying to remember. My eyes fluttered. I held on though, trying to stay suspended in memory. I shot one of the robbers in the ass and I heard the other speaking as he was helping him limp away. Yes, the voice sounded Russian!

Light was burning my eyes. I automatically tried to cover them and jerked my right arm. The pain was dull, but still alarming. My right arm was in a cast. I checked the rest of my body with my left hand. My back hurt a bit, and I had a bandage on the left side of my neck. Other than that, I seemed to be in one piece. Everything floated to my memory at once. Now I felt the ache in every spot. I shot up in my bed and spoke out loud, although I was still feeling groggy, "Han!"

"So, he finally awakes." I jumped at the voice, not realizing I never took in full canvas of the hospital room. It was Larry Lawrence, a representative of the cartel. If he was here, I must be in deep shit. I had a case a few years back.

A girl I had met off a college campus had picked me up to go out. We were smoking a blunt in the Acura she was driving. It was dumb and I never, ever smoked in a moving vehicle since that day. A college security officer smelled the weed as we left the campus. When leaving the campus, you had to stop at a little office like a toll booth, show your ID, and then you're allowed to leave. Same thing when you came in, because so many people that weren't students snuck onto the campus. Usually, lazy campus security waved you on though, because it could turn into a line of traffic. Foolishly, we lit the blunt in the car, but put it out once we got to the checkpoint. Mr. Topflight Security smelled the aroma and let us pass through, then gave the police a description of the car and who was in it. Probably the guy wanted to be a real officer and never made it through the academy.

What I didn't know was Sharlene was driving her brother's car, and he had apparently been blowing her phone up wanting his car back. Sharlene, trying to chill with me of course, ignored the calls from him. "One Time" got behind us and smelled the marijuana, which gave them probable cause, and they ended up searching the car. They found an ounce of cocaine taped under the passenger seat. Obviously, this was why the brother was blowing up Sharlene's phone. He realized he left a package he meant to remove before he let his sister borrow the car.

I was the only one charged. Even given a ridiculously high bond of two hundred thousand dollars, because of us obviously leaving school grounds. Court appointed lawyers will not help you at all. I already had a gun on my record, but thanks to Han's dad, Larry Lawrence made it go away. I felt this issue definitely wasn't. Being best friends with Han was lucrative, but also dangerous. Other than that favor, and our usual drug consignment every two weeks, I never asked for any favors because I knew the game. You never stop owing for the favor. All gangsters keep you in arm's reach.

Yes, Han was my boy since childhood, but I never asked about the family. Never. Larry was here. Something wasn't right about that. Always go with your gut.

"So, to what do I owe the pleasure of this visit? Is Han okay? And where is all my clothes?" I realized I was in a hospital gown. Observing the room, I didn't see my jogging suit, my phone, etc. But if Larry was waiting for me to wake up, he had been there for some time.

"First of all, Yay, Han isn't your main concern. You have new clothes, a new phone, etc. in the closet over there." He nodded towards the bathroom where there was a closet nearby. "You have a firearm by felon charge. I, of course, am representing you and I'll deal with it. Lucky for you it wasn't a stolen gun or some crap you bought off the streets. So many of my other clients buy guns off the street with bodies on them." He shook his head in disgust.

"You can leave whenever you like, but I suggest you get dressed now," he said, plucking something off his expensive shoes, courtesy of the benefits of representing the cartel no doubt. *Not his "other clients" as he put it, as if their money was an afterthought.*

"Get dressed right now? I feel like a train hit me and since you represent me, you could tell me what the hell is going on. They shot Han right in front of me, and I get the feeling I'm being interrogated. I could have died, Larry." I sat up, feeling a bit dizzy, and my anger dulled my pain. It felt good, and he was right. I had to get up and get to the bottom of this.

"Once you're dressed, I will drive you to the Toyota dealership in Halstead Boulevard. Then, you will recite all that happened that night in its entirety. There, you will be instructed on what needs to be done." Larry stood up with his Michael Kors suit on, no doubt shoes to match, all-black with a red tie, and it dawned on me, he looked like Bob Hope in gangsta clothes.

Though he was a white man, about sixty years old, he carried himself with calm, seeming to always know more than you did. Blonde hair slicked back, with green eyes that had seen their share of more than I wanted to know. He always put me on game though. When Larry said something in a sarcastic manner, there was always a deeper meaning behind it.

I saw a bottle on the table beside me, my name on it with painkillers in capsule form. I popped two and stopped Larry as he was stepping out the room. I assumed he was allowing me to dress in private.

"Hey, Larry, who the hell are we going to see at the Toyota dealership? Did my BMW get towed or something?" I sat while balancing myself as I got out the bed. Larry had just slid his phone back into the side pocket of his suit. He looked at me as if I'd asked a dumb question.

"Once you're dressed, we are going to see Mr. Han Che." And then he shut the door. Now it all made sense. Larry was my personal escort and no doubt had just by phone let Han Che know we would soon be there. Shit was about to hit the fan.

Chapter 3

Big Dawg Status

Signing all the necessary paperwork was not my style. I got dressed and amazingly, my phone still had "L.L." as one of my contacts in my new Boost Mobile phone. It was better than my old phone. I got dressed and texted, "I'm coming out."

I walked out the hospital, and I heard Kevin Gates rapping, "I got two phones, one for the plus and one for the hoes..." Then I realized it was my phone, so I answered it.

"Yay, I'm in a gold Lexus LS 400. Hurry, I have things to do." The phone clicked dead in my ear. As he hung up, I heard a horn beep twice. I went towards the sound and got in the car. We rode for a while with nothing but Teena Marie playing on the radio. She was talking "Square Business." Kind of ironic. Our business came in squares.

We reached the Toyota dealership. There was a sign that said, "Out to lunch. Back in an hour." We traveled to the back of the dealership. It was dreary outside and a bit gloomy. I was hungry as hell, wondering when I last ate. I'd been out of it a day and a half, let the date on my new phone tell it. I looked around and saw a big, twelve-car garage, which we were approaching.

"You ridin back here like you own the place, Larry." He seemed familiar with the setting.

"Of course," he replied, "I'm a lawyer, so I had a part. Han Che, if you must know, became the owner a month ago." He always had a knowing grin, and I hated it.

"Okay, this is far as I go. I'll let you know of your court date, if you have one. So, good luck to you. Yay, oh by the way, garage number five is where you'll see Han Che." I nodded my thanks and got out the car. I threw my hoodie on my head as Larry was making a U-turn to leave.

All of a sudden, the garage door on number five came up. An all-black Maybach came out of the garage right beside me. The window cracked and Han Che's voice, with its laid-back demeanor sounded cheerful, but was masked with venom. "Let's take a ride and talk like men." Then the window rolled up. I took a deep breath and got in the expensive vehicle. The curtains on the windows were pulled closed. I had never been in one, but it felt like money.

I thought, *how much is Han Che worth? Fifty million, a hundred million...* No one knew. He lit a Cuban and cracked the window just a little bit.

"About two days ago, Han met up with you and Polo. Things went wrong." He held his hands up. "Hey, it happens. Now, I can't find Polo just yet. But I need the wrong to be right." He clapped his hands and rubbed them together. "Then, we clean up the mess that was made. Money first. The vendetta is settled in time." He smiled and playfully slapped me on the arm. I was lost at the moment. Han was dead, so why was he not grieving? As if he read my mind, he leaned toward me. His eyes looked mean, and I realized then I was talking to a killer. He gritted his teeth with anger as he spoke.

"I never wanted Han in this shit, but he refused. What could I say, when I'm in the life? I don't need to go to the morgue. Arrangements are already done. My son died when my wife, Charlotte, died. So, with that said, you will right this wrong." He leaned back, playing with his pinkie ring.

"Yo, Mr. Han Che, look... I'll get the twenty-five bricks, or I'll just pay the three hundred and seventy-five grand owed, soon as I get situated. I mean, I almost died myself. I need to find out what the hell is going on." I rubbed my head. I had a throbbing headache, so I reached for my painkillers. All of a sudden, a Desert Eagle was pointed at my head. We looked each other in the eyes as I spoke as calmly as I ever had in my life.

"Mr. Che, I got painkillers in my pocket. I'm pulling them out. Your son, for all I know, died in my arms. I still have a gun charge for your son." I opened my hand, still not taking my eyes off his. I showed him the pill bottle. He glanced down and put the gun back in the cigar case. I took a deep breath.

"Am I in some kind of damn trouble I don't know about? My godfather just pulled a gun on me and put it in my face." I was heated.

Han Che tossed me his phone and when I looked at it, there was a message from Han. It said, "I have a hundred girls at my hotel room. I'm inviting Yay to help me with the girls!" I dropped the damn phone, trying to figure out what was happening. I picked the phone back up, read it again, and then handed it back to Han Che. The code was basically saying Han was hitting me with a hundred bricks. The fucked-up part was we were only meeting for twenty-five. I never take consignment. I pay for my birds, then I fly away. That way there is no issue about money owed.

"Han Che, come on. I've never handled over fifty birds." The nickname of a kilo was called a bird. "That message isn't correct. I don't know what happened! That night we pulled up, waited, and Han pulled up. I got out, and he opened the trunk. Then from nowhere, three guys masked up, swarmed us." My head was spinning. Now I knew why we were having this meeting. Han was dead. Polo was MIA. So, I was obviously responsible for a hundred bricks, WTF! I was calculating my stash in my head. I had a little over two hundred and fifty thousand, plus some jewelry I never wore.

A hundred birds at thirteen thousand a pop was one-point-five million, easy.

I turned my head at the sound of glasses and Han Che pulled a bottle out of a sparkly case. It was cognac in a rare cask, Louis XIII, which was expensive. I had a homie who made it out the hood playing football. He had one in Jupiter, FL, eating at a restaurant called The Woods. The Louis XIII was available at seventeen hundred per shot, and this nigga got the whole bottle. Holding that shit like a forty, he poured us both a glass, held it up to me to toast. "To righting a wrong." He threw his drink back. I did the same. It was so good, smooth. It helped with the pain in my right arm, helped me move my shoulder too. He tapped the hood of the car with his knuckles. The car slowed to a stop.

"I don't know Polo like I know you, but I know it wasn't your fault. So, you tell Polo what you want. Regardless, Han came to meet you. Now, unfortunately, you owe me. You have a week." He relit his Cuban, and that was the end of our conversation.

Once I was out the car, I realized I was only two blocks from my apartment. Again, Kevin Gates rapped about having two phones. I answered, "Hello."

"OMG! Baby, I'm glad you're okay. The police said go to the hospital after I got questioned. Then they gave me a hard time because we weren't married." She was out of breath. "Where are you anyway?"

"First of all, how you get this number?" I said, walking towards my apartment.

"Larry gave me the number. He said to call you after I saw you get out of a fly ass car." Then she was quiet. "Um, that is Han Che's Maybach, isn't it?"

"Yes, it is. If you saw me getting out of a car, then you must be in my apartment," I said.

"Um, No nigga, *our* apartment. I do have a key. I been here waiting to get news if you were okay. A nice doctor told me after I called a thousand times, your left side of your neck was grazed and a bullet went through your right shoulder," she said, sounding upset. I told her I was coming up as I got to the elevator of the apartment complex. She buzzed me in, and it made me thankful. It was extra, but you couldn't get in unless you were buzzed in. No one really knew I lived there. Han Che had been doing his homework. Milk Marie met me in the hallway. She almost jumped on me, until she noticed the cast on my right arm.

We kissed and hugged, then we went inside. It felt good to be there. I had to get my thoughts clear. Milk Marie was walking past me in boy shorts and a tight wife beater. I couldn't front. Milk Marie wasn't exactly wifey material, but her body was banging! Looking like a thotty Selena Gomez. Her hair was pitch black and down to her ass. We had never tried the girlfriend-boyfriend level. Never worked and we just existed. I liked the sex, no doubt, but Milk Marie had a reputation for being loose.

She was sexy enough to where it was what it was. Her kids were with her mom, and she kept that world to herself. She went to the kitchen and poured us both a glass of Grey Goose. She said on the couch beside me in the living room. I downed the glass, and the burn helped my arm. I got up and brought the bottle in the living room. I felt her eyes on me. I poured another shot of the clear liquid Jeezy said was holy water. I turned to her stare.

"I'm sorry about Han. I know that was your friend. I thought you were both..." She took a deep breath, "I was scared I was hit. Some bullets hit your car. The BMW is at the impound. I got the number on a sticky note on the fridge. Polo hit my phone with only one text. He said for you to get at him." She sipped her drink, twirling her hair, "Are you okay, baby?" She moved over to me and massaged my neck a little, trying to be careful not to hit my shoulder or my arm. It felt good, and I could smell the Chanel No5 on her skin. The Grey Goose had me buzzing. We talked a bit about all that could have gone wrong.

"No one knew we were meeting but me and Han. I didn't even tell Polo until I pulled up. Polo and Han are always bickering, so I usually don't have Polo with me. When I told him where I was going, he just shrugged and stayed in the back seat." I kept rewinding that night in my head as Milk Marie's massage began to relax me.

"I got out the car and walked toward Han. Then Han nodded to Polo. I looked back, and Polo was nodding back. I asked him when he and Polo had become buddy-buddy. Then he popped the trunk, two duffel bags were inside, and Han took then out of the trunk. Then out of nowhere, three dudes moved on us. We had been meeting there for two years at that spot. So, where was the leak? What was I missing? But I did hear one of them speaking in Russian, while helping the guy I shot in the ass."

I took another sip of the Goose and felt Milk Marie's hands caress my dick through my jogging pants. She was biting her lip, looking at me. This was our connection. We were both sexual savages, but I prolonged her lust only for a short while. I told her to get up, look in the kitchen drawer, and bring me some big scissors. I got some old newspapers off the counter and spread them out. I wanted to do this while the liquor still had me.

I used to play football. I had a shoulder harness that would at least support my arm but keep it looser. We cut at the cast for about an hour with debris all on the top of the counter. It was off my arm. My arm was a bit limp, but I could still move my fingers. Milk Marie wrapped my shoulder in a bandage I had from days of basketball. Then slipped on the harness with ease. The elastic felt better than the cast. We cleaned up then I rolled a blunt of Triple OG in a Garcia Vega. I always had a stash to smoke.

I went to the bedroom and turned on the big screen TV. The movie *Belly* was on. I flopped on the bed, then sat up on the big pillows on the bed. Milk Marie had brought the bottle and glasses in as well. I watched her and damn, she was pretty. The camel toe in the boy shorts was poking out like new rims on a foreign. Her breasts were suffocating in the wife beater she wore.

I lit the blunt, laughing when DMX grabs Keisha and yells, "Listen, listen." I inhaled the smoke and as I exhaled, I kept thinking of Han. *Damn, my nigga dead, and I got to get one-point-five million up in a week.* Life is so crazy. One minute I owed no one, and now it felt like I owed the world. First thing on my list was to find Polo and try to get a line on the niggas that jacked us.

I felt Milk Marie take the blunt out of my hand. She didn't really smoke like that. So, I took it as a sign she was horny. When she got the blunt, she put the lit part in her mouth. Then she climbed on my best and blew me a gun from the blunt. The smoke transferred from her mouth to mine. I laid back, feeling the effects of the cognac from earlier, the Goose and the weed. I kicked my Jordans off. She pulled my jogging pants and boxers off.

She purred like a cat, crawling between my legs on the bed. "Is this all for me, daddy?" she said with a cute giggle, as she stroked my manhood up and down, licking her lips.

I looked at her under the hoods of my eyelids, as high as the Eiffel Tower. I sat up a little more, trying to get my arm comfortable. "Hey, baby, can I ask you something?" as I drifted off. Milk Marie kept stroking me.

"What, daddy?" she said in her exotic, giggly voice.

"Why do they call you Milk Marie instead of just Shay-la?" I said, biting my lips as I felt her lick all over the head. Then she blew her breath on it, still stroking me a little faster now. Then she slowed it up. Damn, she was a beast. Her raised head looked up at me from between my legs, and she made a nasty face as she stared at me and then back at my dick. Then she laughed as if I'd asked a crazy question, and she took all of my dick in her mouth. She was deep throating. I couldn't speak at all. I was pulling on her long hair.

Finally, she came up for air and said, "You know damn well why they call me Milk Marie." Then with no mercy, she looked me in my eyes as she deep throated my manhood.

While Milk Marie was living up to her name, I was trying to figure out who had robbed us. Right now, my body felt like it was trapped in a very moist vacuum. I nodded to her lips smacking. Somebody had betrayed us, but who...

Chapter 4

All or Nothing...

After I woke up from Milk Marie's inviting lips, I leaned up with satin burgundy sheets over me from my waist down. I smelled coffee, and it was just what I needed. I leaned up. "Fuck!" I snarled. I took a deep breath, slipped my Polo boxers back on, and pulled on my jogging pants. I slipped my feet in my Jordans and popped two painkillers.

"Baby, you okay in there?" I heard Milk Marie yell from the kitchen.

"Yo, I'm good. Roll up, and do we have any more Goose?" My shoulder was sore as shit, but I could move it. I felt the painkillers dulling the ache.

I walked into the kitchen and saw a bottle of Goose, a glass, and Milk Marie throwing that long hair out her face while pouring herself a cup of mud. I noticed she had my coffee mug, which read on the front, "Good things come to those who hustle." I bought it in South Carolina, on my way to Savannah, GA. Her coffee mug had a Hello Kitty logo on it with lipstick prints all over it. She had Hello Kitty tattooed on her left foot. She always complained it itched, but it was a sexy tattoo. As if on cue, she was rubbing her right foot with her left.

"I tell you, this tattoo stays itching. So, what exactly do you plan to do?" Milk Marie said, looking like she could be another sister in the Kardashian family. I just truly noticed she was actually dressed and looking fly. She had on a Fendi fitted dress that came to her knees, hugging her curves. She also had Fendi shades on her head. The shades were the same dark green as the dress, and they had the word Fendi spelled in big white letters on the side. She had on high heels that spelled the word, "Fendi." The shit looked dope. I couldn't believe I met this chic in the hood, bouncing from dude to dude, riding around with a bunch of thotty white chics drinking five o'clock cheap liquor.

See, Milk Marie had kids early. I think she was sixteen years old. I mean, of course she dated white boys at first, but I guess once a brotha hit it, it was a wrap. But she had her demons. Her first baby daddy had two kids by her. She dropped out of school and tried humping a nigga that smoked weed and played PlayStation all day. You know that shit gets played, even for the chics just looking to fuck.

Somebody robbed them while she was pregnant with a second baby. Ran up in the crib and they put a bat to her big stomach, basically threatening to go Babe Ruth if her baby daddy, Freddie, didn't come off the pounds of weed. But the nigga was lame, and he only had four ounces in the fridge and a thousand in cash on him. The lick wasn't what the robbers thought, so they kicked Freddie's ass while Milk Marie and her son watched. When she told me this months ago, she said she knew the robbers and he did too. The mask didn't disguise their voices.

It was Day Day, Tron and a nigga named Dree. Now let me tell you after that, she was cold to the nigga Freddie. After she had the second baby, their relationship was rough. They were always broke, living with friends because her mom didn't like her messing with black guys, but the grandkids were so cute, her mom just accepted her daughter's fetish.

But she refused to let her come home, even took the kids from Marie and Freddie. They were both sniffing coke. She had two more kids, not by him, but the dumb nigga kept dealing with her. Shorty blamed all the bullshit on that night. "If he had some backbone, he would have handled that. But being he knew the three clowns that robbed us, he acted pussy. So, I got tired of it," she said one night when we were chilling.

Obviously, Dree came up on her one night. She was hanging out. Her claim was she was drunk and wanted to hurt his feelings. So, she fucked Dree, which was one of the niggas that robbed them. Freddie never fucked with her after that. Plus, her mom had custody of the kids. That was years before I met her, but it was still foul.

I mean, Milk Marie was sexy. She was bisexual and we had our share of threesomes. But I could never make her my girl. Yet, she had been with me for about eight months now. We had our fallouts. She was in a homeless shelter when I bailed her out of jail. When I dropped her off, as I drove down the road, I saw her turn from the shelter and walk back down the street. It was 1:00 am. I turned around.

"Yo, Shayla, I thought that's where you lived, shawty," I said from the window of my old skool '83 Marquis on twenty-four's. I usually didn't drive it like that because of unwanted attention. But the BMW I bought wasn't ready yet. I learned my lesson about putting big rims on cars. Shit is a police magnet. She stopped walking and let out a loud sigh.

"Look, that's not my home. Okay? It's a shelter. I thought you had drove off."

"I was, but I saw you in my rearview mirror, and it's late," I said, pulling into a closed CVS parking lot. It was summer then, but the nights would get chilly. Shorty had a wife beater on, little ass shorts, and some flip flops on her feet. I knew she had to be cold.

"Look, um..." she said, rubbing her forehead.

"My name is Yay," I said looking around, ready to get out that part of town. Po-Po was hot in that area, and my car looking like it came out a T.I. video at 1:00 in the morning was not good.

"Okay, well look... um, Yay... My mom won't let me come home. She got my kids, and funds are tight at the moment. It's past curfew to get into the shelter. I appreciate you getting me out, but I'm hung over. I got left on the highway by an asshole I wouldn't fuck. So, if you'll excuse me," she said, beginning to walk off.

"Why don't you stay with me? I mean, just for tonight, and I'll bring you back in the am. You cool with that?" I looked at her. I mean, really looked at her. I knew that look. The world was whipping her ass. I knew the feeling, but shorty was pretty tough. Long ass hair, breasts were big though, and the ass in those little shorts was nice. She did have a big ass nose, but it gave her a certain look.

"So, you bail me out and now you think I'm going to go home with you, nigga? I just told you what I went through," she said, throwing her hair to one side of her face.

"First off, you still a white girl. I don't care how many black guys you've hung with or fucked. Never call me a nigga again. Second, I'm used to pussy. Not my fault you been around so many asses. My bad, real is not what you used to." I was tuning Meek Millz up with his rapping, he was a boss. I was about to leave this broad when my nigga Patron hit my phone up.

"Yo, what it do, playa?" I said, putting my classic in drive.

"What up, Yayo? Hey, man, why you in Bucktown? I just passed you and the Po-Po kind of hot out there. You might want to relocate Shirley with that burgundy paint job and big rims. I see you, but it hot, homie. I just was hitting your line to keep you on point. Peace."

I was driving off, listening to the music when I looked in the passenger seat and realized Shayla was sitting there. I didn't even hear her get in the car. She was facing the window, shivering a little. I reached in the back seat and gave her my Jordan hoodie. She slipped it on and pulled her long hair out. She looked cute as hell in my hoodie.

"So, you bringing me back in the morning, right?" she said, facing the windows, not even looking my way.

"Fo sho. I got you." Then I tensed up. She must have noticed because she looked over the dashboard. There was a roadblock, and I wasn't dirty. But it was late as hell. Bucktown area was crackhead-ville. I turned out the line of people waiting to get their license checked. I had none. As I was turning down the other road, she tapped my arm. I looked over at her.

"Yo, pull over and let me drive," she said as I pulled over. She crawled over me as we switched places. She must have felt the bulge in my pants. I had been looking at her thighs while driving. Shayla blushed and soon as she pulled off, the cops are off behind us. Once the officer approached, Shayla pulled her license out. When he went back to his car to look at it, she turned to me. "Is this really your car, because my night has been bad enough," she said, eyes pleading the car was legit.

"I have an aunt in Virginia. Her name is Nancy Baxter." I leaned back. "Don't worry, everything is legit. Plus, I never smoke in my cars or have anything in them." The light came out of nowhere. He gave her the license, then put the flashlight on me. Then walked around the car, and then back to Shayla.

"Ms. Johnson, do you know who owns this car?" he said, chewing gum like it the last damn piece on Earth.

"Yes, sir. It's my boyfriend's aunt's car, Officer. I am thinking about buying it, because she doesn't like the tires."

He looked at her, looked at the car and said, "Well, it's an eighty-three, which is a classic. Hope you get her a good deal." He said to me, "Go home, stay out of Bucktown this late, or you won't have those rims or tires."

When he left, I felt I was holding my breath. Real redneck but Shayla handled it.

"So, if this is your car, I guess you doing your thing, huh... So, are you really nice like this all the time?" she said, with the wind whipping her hair around. "You always trying to help people?"

I told her where the apartment was downtown. She knew the area. Once we got to the apartment, I said, "I've been thinking through things, so I will do what I can if I can relate to any struggle. But something about you... I just feel compelled to help you." Then I looked her up and down. "Plus, it don't hurt that you a cutie too."

"Oh, you think so? Well, I can't front. You fine. I just not trying to gas you up. I mean, I see you," she said, twirling her hair, "but I know you got a girl."

"Naw. No girlfriend as a matter of fact. No girl, until now, has ever been in my apartment. Just my boy, Patron, knows this spot."

"Why you all by yourself for, you seem like a good dude. Shit, I've dated guys that don't have a house or car. So why the hermit routine?" she said, looking around the apartment.

"Trust," I said, rolling a blunt. "Less is more, boo. I'm low radar. Feel me?"

She laughed a cute, loud laugh that made her seem less street. "Bye, bye. You got, as the cop said, 'a classic,'" she said, imitating his redneck voice, "on twenty-fours out there. Yeah, real low radar."

"Okay, it was my first car, and I have another that's less attention. But I'm all about being low key."

I showed her the bathroom and gave her Polo boxers and an old LRG shirt. After she came out the bathroom, I went and showered. I came out with my towel wrapped around me. She was sitting in the living room flipping through channels, but her eyes were drinking me in. My workout game was on point, and my frame was chiseled. But she was cute, and I never had company like that. So, yes, I was flexing on shorty.

I threw on some Hilfiger pajamas while puffing on that loud. I stuck my head out my bedroom door. "My fridge got juice, milk etc., in it. So, I guess I'll see you in the am. Thanks for driving for me. I'm sure I would have bumped into that roadblock after I thought I was dropping you off," I said, pulling my dreads in a ponytail.

"Hey, why did that guy call your car Shirley on the phone? And what's your real name? Since now you know mine."

"Okay, well, my mom's name was Shirley, but I was adopted so I never met her. Years later, my aunt found me and that's how I found out my mom's name. And if you must know, my name is Seemiyun," I said, slipping a Hilfiger tee on.

"Seemiyun? Sound like a white boy's name, but I like it. I don't go by Shayla. All my friends call me Milk Marie."

"But you said I got a weird name. I see you, Milk Marie. I reached out to give her dap. But she surprised me by getting up and giving me a hug. She smelled good and she felt good.

I could feel her breath on my chest when she said, "Yo, for real, Yay, thank you for letting me crash." I was six-three, and she was like five feet tall. I tried to pass her the blunt, but she said shit gives her panic attacks. So, I told her if she liked to sip, I kept Goose on deck in the fridge.

I went to my bedroom and passed out on the bed. I had a long day, and I was ready to get the BMW from the dealership. I was up to five keys a week and I felt I was ready for ten, but I told Han, "No consignment anymore, now that I'm up. I buy my own work." My nigga, Patron, was moving half of it and the streets were thirsty. I was grinning as I snuggled into my pillow.

"You always smile to yourself when you get ready for bed?" Milk Marie said beside my bed as I jumped a little.

"Damn, girl! You a ninja or something? So, you always sneak up on people like that?" I sat up against the pillows. She had two glasses of Goose in her hand.

"I cannot sleep. Take a shot with me." I took the glass and threw back the shot. I felt her eyes on me. Then I felt her hands touch mine, but it was to take the glass. Her touch stayed for a while when she took the glass. She scooted over and looked at me, biting her bottom lip. She grabbed my shirt and pulled me to her. The kiss was nice and long with a lot of tongue. Once we finally stopped kissing, she said, "Damn, that was nice."

With her head down a bit, she said, "Guys are assholes and I'm not an angel. I haven't met anyone that didn't want to hit it then quit it. But," looking up at me, "you cool as fuck, and I had nowhere to go tonight. You didn't even try to come at me sexually. That turned me on, honestly." She took a deep breath. "What I'm trying to say is, when I was in the living room, I thought of you giving me your hoodie in the car, when I was cold, no one does that shit anymore."

"I do and that's just me, ma. You know?" I said, pushing her hair to the side. "This me every day. No fugayzee," I said, leaning back on the bed.

"And I like your lips too. Look, this might sound dumb, but I imagined being your girlfriend. I'm used to getting hit on. So, this is new to me, but…" she looked at me with a sincere look, "Can I act like I'm your girlfriend and you're my man? I don't know about tomorrow, but I want you tonight." Then she pushed me back on the bed. We were pulling at each other's clothes and kissing like animals. She kissed my neck, then my chest, and she licked both my nipples. Never had that done before. I was bone-hard by the time she got to my stomach. I had my hands in her hair. Damn, her hair was long, and it was sliding down my body and tickling me, along with her soft kisses, making me shake as she went lower and lower.

"Hey, can I ask you something?" I said, biting my lips as she kissed my manhood.

"Yeah," she said between pecks all over.

"Why do they call you Milk Marie, boo?" I said as she stroked my dick.

She flung her hair back and grinned at me like I asked a crazy question. "Ummm… I could tell you, but how about I show you. I mean, you are my knight in shining armor." She didn't say anything else. She was devouring me and had sloppy spit all over my dick. She seemed to be whispering to it like she was having a conversation. "Mmm, yeah, you a big boy, mmm give it to me," she said, between licks.

I thought, *Milk Marie, yeah that makes sense now.*

"Yay, Yay! I hate when you do that daydreaming shit when I'm trying to talk to you," she said, pouring another cup of coffee.

"My bad, ma," I said, walking up to her and grabbing the cup of coffee, then putting a nice amount of Grey Goose in it. I downed half of it, then drank the rest. I repeated the process and felt better. "Now, what were you saying?"

"I said... What exactly do you plan to do? Han Che really think you got a hundred bricks? I don't know all your business, but even that don't make sense to me." She said, looking worried, "Is Han even having a funeral? I don't know how the Chinese do all that."

"Han Che told me arrangements were made. Give me the number Polo texted you from. If I can get up with him, then I can get to the bottom of this. I know Han and Polo had issues, but we all were boys. I just knew Han longer," I said, sipping my spiked coffee.

Once I called and someone picked up, and it sounded like a female. "Hello," then I heard mumbling, like arguing. "I'm expecting a call, Tawana. Damn, girl. If you don't know the number, why answer it? I told you let me answer it, damn."

"It's my damn phone, but it better not be no bitch." I heard the female voice say.

"Why would I have a bitch call your phone, Tawana? Cut the shit." Polo said with an attitude, "Yo, who is this, and how you get this number?"

"Yo, shit has hit the fan. I need you to link up with me at the park by the waterfront," I said, moving my shoulder up and down. The Goose and coffee was working.

"Oh shit, Yay! I was told you were laid up with bullets in you. I had to bounce, man. So many cops came. I was in this old lady backyard hiding damn near until the sun came up," Polo said, still trying to quiet Tawana. "Yo! Larry, a spooky old white dude, somehow got a message to Tawana to get up with you. So, I text Milk Marie phone from Tawana's cell and threw my cell away. Hey, is um, is Han..."

"Yeah, man. Han dead, Po," I said, still not believing it myself.

"Fuck! Fuck!" I heard Polo yell. "Man, he was a thorn in my side, but he was still people. So, what's the plan?"

"We find the niggas that jacked us, and somehow get Han Che his bread. I'll explain it to you. I'll be there in an hour," I said to Polo.

"Owe Han Che? Nigga, I thought you stop doing consignment a long time ago. You the man scoring thirty jump shots a game." Meaning how many bricks I moved by myself.

"Tell me something I don't know. I'll explain it to you face-to-face. I'm off this one," I said to Polo.

"One," Polo replied back, then hung up.

I went to my bedroom, told Milk Marie to wait in the living room. I turned the shower on and took a quick one. Then I put on some dark Levi jeans, my Timbs and an all-black, long sleeve shirt. I didn't want my shoulder harness to show. I kept the shower running just for sound. I pushed a button in my closet. A side panel slid down, and I smiled at my personal arsenal.

I had five AKs, three Uzis, a few nines and another Desert Eagle. I even had night vision goggles and two grenades. I had a weird feeling this might come in handy one day. I knew a retired arms dealer who loved cocaine. So, these were a few gifts when he didn't want to part with cash. Was a nice trade for me. I even had two AK-15's. I picked a 357 Magnum, and the Desert Eagle, which was seven inches and four pounds. It had seventeen, with one in the head. I pushed the button so the wall panel would go back to where it was. I put on two holsters, one for my left shoulder, and a hip holster.

I put on my leather jacket. Glad it was chilly outside with November around the corner. I looked in the mirror in the bathroom after clearing off the fog. I looked at my reflection. "All or nothing, Yay," I said to myself.

I walked in the living room, smacked Milk Marie on the ass, and we were on our way out the door. I told her we were taking her black Tahoe, being my BMW was in the impound.

Milk Marie said, after bringing the truck to life, "Where are we going, baby, after you talk to Polo?"

I leaned back, turning up 50 Cent on her radio. The song played, "Many men. Many, many, men, many men, wish death upon me, Lord. I don't smile no more, don't look to the sky no more – have mercy on me, have mercy on my soul, somewhere my heart turned cold."

I patted her on her thick thighs and said, "We going hunting!"

I thought of Han, and how we grew up together once he moved here. I thought of Polo and how we linked up years ago after meeting in prison. Honestly, my dude, Terence "T.J." Jackson, AKA Patron, grew up with me at the orphanage. We were much younger then. But as I listened to 50 Cent talk about his many enemies, I was wondering who was wishing death upon me. I mean, I've had my share of niggas trying to test me. But I put in my work, the reason why I was low key now. Broke niggas make noise. Rich niggas make moves. That was my motto. I had to find this snake and fast. I missed Han, but I wasn't trying to join him.

Chapter 5

Looking For Answers...

We got a little bite to eat, then drove past the park twice, thirty minutes early. Just to make sure everything was okay, and no one was looking. Polo fled, I dig that, but how did anyone know to be there that night? Did Han really plan to give me a hundred bricks? I didn't tell Polo until I was on my way to meet Han. Something was bugging me, a clue I knew but hadn't realized. Milk Marie hit a speed bump, shaking me out of my thoughts. We came to the park a little over an hour, just to be safe.

A few kids were playing and about four cars were parked in the parking lot. I could see the angle of three roads coming and going. Public, kids around, and it was neutral ground. Don't know why I felt like this though, me and Polo were cool. My gut kept gnawing at me. For now, I would play cool. A week wasn't a big window for so much at stake.

I got a text saying, "I guess this your new line. I'm in a white Bronco." I looked around and saw the truck. We parked on the other end of where it was. There was a gazebo at the far end of the park. I saw Tawana and her daughter, Crystal, playing. I only met Tawana a few times. Polo had different chics, so I could never get to know them. Tawana was the most constant. Crystal was eight years old. Polo never took a test, but it was his kid. Why he never took the test, I don't know. Maybe because when he would be gone a day or two, she would threaten to get the test. She was lame, because the kid was eight now, but it wasn't my business.

I texted, "Go to the gazebo." I pocketed my phone and told Milk Marie I would be right back. She was watching a DVD of *Meet the Kardashians* in the dashboard of the truck.

"I'm good. Just be safe and remember, it's kids out here," she said, glancing at me.

"Why you looking at me like that?" I said, adjusting my holster, about to get out the Tahoe.

"Bae, we passed the park twice, and I know you packing. Just be cool. I know how smart you are. You'll figure this out, right?" she said, putting the TV on mute.

"I don't know, Milk. I mean, someone set me up. I'm the only one dealing with a package I never got. It's bullshit and my boy dead. So, trust me when I do figure this out, niggas going to bleed. Period. No maxi pad," I said, getting out the truck.

It was chilly out, but still a nice day. I could see a little bit of my breath as I walked towards the gazebo. I saw Polo get to it before me. Once I was inside, we dapped up, then we sat down.

"Bruh, WTF happened that night? Those dudes had Uzis and came out of nowhere. What's going on, Yay?" Polo said, shaking his head.

"Man, I don't know. All I know is three fools got the drop on us. Han is dead, and I'm in debt with Han Che for a lot of squares I don't know I can corner. It's the money or the squares."

"Damn, how much money, Yay?" Polo said, shaking his head.

Too much to count, I wanted to say. "I just need to pay Han Che or get the bricks back. But how the fuck I'm going to do that when I don't even know who hit us?" I said, frustrated, rotating my shoulder.

"So, how you feeling? I know that shit hurt like hell," Polo said, taking out a flask sipping from it, then handing it to me. I took a deep swig, swallowed, and almost doubled over.

"Yo, what the fuck is this?" I said, rubbing my throat looking at the bottle.

"Hennessy, nigga. I forgot you like that holy water," Polo said, taking another sip. It did warm me up though.

"Like Jeezy said, 'My partner on brown, but you know I'm on white," I said. "But look, I need you to find out if anyone trying to sell a nice quantity of work. If I'm lucky, the dope is still in the city," I added, drinking one last swig from the flask, balling my face up.

"Yo, I know you got plenty of dough put up. Why don't you just bounce? Why sit here and play Dick Tracy? Han Che makes niggas magically disappear," Polo said, waving at Crystal playing with another little girl.

"Bounce? Bounce? Yo, Polo, what I look like? One of my friends got smoked. We both almost got killed." I was shaking my head. "Fuck running. Somehow, I feel I got set up. So, I need to know. Are you with me, or what?"

"You don't even got to ask, partner. You know my gun go off. I've never talked to or dealt with Han, but he gone so why risk your life?" Polo said, leaning back.

I stood up because Polo was pissing me off. That could have been any one of us that got popped. I had made up my mind. I was going to grind my ass off. Get Han Che what I could and pray I could get an extension. Han Che was always cool with me, being that me and Han were close. That's why his heartless demeanor in the Maybach had me feeling some kind way. But I know in this life, better to be pissed off than pissed on. I had a decent life. I was even part owner of the E-City Housing Duplex I lived in.

I accomplished that when me and Milk Marie had a fall-out. Confusing as it may sound, I "loved" Milk Marie. I just know I couldn't afford to be "in love" with her. It's like having a good friend that was good at fucking you. I was never at the apartment back then and a few days went by. I came in the apartment, and she was on the couch. Shit like that was exactly why I was like, *fuck love.*

I had missed her, and it pissed me off that I felt vulnerable. I put a wall up. I was different from then on. But what I can say I wasn't the police. I wasn't handcuffing nobody. Attachment made you soft. I was attached to money. I was alone a lot growing up. I could always depend on the guy in the mirror. I never wanted to count on anyone once my bands were right.

"If you don't want to do this, then don't. You got my new number and stay on point. You never know if those three fools might want to finish what they started."

"I hear you, Yay, but they came for the coke. Plain and simple. Shit, for all we know, Han had enemies. He could have been followed or anything…" Polo said, standing as we both walked out the gazebo.

"You could be right, but just get at me. I got to go see a man about a horse." I dapped him again. "Broke niggas make noise."

"But rich niggas make moves," Polo said, walking toward Tawana.

I hopped in the truck and told Milk Marie to take me to the DMV. There I paid fifteen hundred for all of my old fines, and a three-hundred-dollar reinstatement fee. Some sexy ass, light-skinned older lady told me she could have my license in a week, even though it was supposed to take a month for everything to clear. So, she got five hundred extra for that service, and she hinted to me she had other services as a bonus.

She looked like an older version of Tisha Campbell, you know, the chic that plays Gina on *Martin*. I gave her my info, and she walked me back out to the spacious waiting room where Milk Marie was waiting. The lady said her name was Shavonda and to please come get my identification in a week. I promised I would, and I saw Milk Marie walk out while rolling her eyes. I sensed attitude, so once in the truck I asked, "Why you rolling your eyes and acting all bougie for? Thought you'd be happy I got my license. Now you don't have to drive me everywhere." Rolling a blunt in the passenger seat. I wasn't in the mood for this Nicki Minaj, Meek Mill bullshit.

"Well, maybe I liked riding you around. I thought you had to wait thirty days, then take the test," she said, pulling out the parking lot a bit too fast.

"Yo, Milk Marie, don't start that hot shit, have twelve on us," I said, almost dropping the blunt.

"I guess that old red bitch with the big booty you like helped, huh?" Imitating the lady, "Please come back for your identification," Milk Marie said. "Damn old slut. These hoes don't care if you are with a nigga or not," she said with attitude, smacking her teeth.

"Girl, what I tell you about that nigga shit?" I said, pulling on the sour dee.

"Umm, niggggaaahhhh," Milk Marie said with a girly attitude. "When I'm fucking and sucking that dick, and you beating this pussy up, nigga make it cum, I don't hear you correcting me," she said, her lips curled up. I blew loud smoke in her face. It always made her mad.

"Damn… stop, Yay," she said, rolling the window down, trying to slap the blunt out of my hand.

"Girl, that's different. When I'm on my Mr. Marcus shit, that's a no-flex zone." I looked at her. "What's got you all pissy? I wasn't mad at you when you were M.I.A. for days. Didn't say nothing, plus niggas holla at you, no matter if I'm around or not. You know I missed…" I just stopped talking.

"Look, I told you I was at my mother's seeing the kids. She barely let me stay those few days. Regardless of how we've been, you know I care about you."

I couldn't hear her. I was calling Patron to avoid this conversation. She took the hint and put in her Nicki Minaj CD *Pinkprint*.

"Yo, what's good? Speak to me," Patron said with confidence.

"Damn, you answer any number that hits your line, playa. What's the business, my dude?" I said, glancing at Milk Marie who obviously still had an attitude.

"Oh, shit! What's good, Yay? Boy I heard you were laid up. What's the science, my gee?" Patron replied.

"My dude, I got a snake in my garden. So obviously, I need to keep my grass cut. Yuh feel me? Where you at?"

"I'm out Buck, chillin with this little chic making plays, feel me? But yo, the hood need you. I'm 'bout dry and I didn't get them thang-thangs from you, my gee," said Patron.

Patron was young, black, and hood down all the way to the stop sign. He lives to hustle. When we were kids, he used to sell candy and my nigga had kids lined up like they were waiting for the school bus. Times like this, I'm glad he was on my team.

"Yo, I'm not coming out Bucktown, but I tell you what... Meet me at the mall. I'll be parked by Burke's Outlet," I said, throwing the blunt out the window.

"Say no more. So, is everything good? Do you know who shot you?" Patron asked.

"I'll talk to you about that once we face-to-face. How long will you be?" I said, running my fingers through Milk Marie's hair. She tried to keep an attitude, but I licked my lips at her and blew a kiss. She rolled her eyes, but she didn't seem as mad. She wasn't usually like that. Wonder what was up with her.

"Give me about thirty minutes and I'll be there for sho," Patron said.

"No doubt, my nigga. Broke niggas make noise," I said.

"While rich niggas make moves," Patron replied then hung up.

"Yo, Milk, park by those woods behind the mall by the dumpster right quick," I said, popping a painkiller. She didn't ask why, just followed instructions. Once we parked, I told her to keep the engine running. The Tahoe was spacious. It came with three rows of seats. I let the second row of seats down until it was a flat surface. I pulled her in the back.

"Yay, what you doing?" she said, both Fendi heels kicked off. Once she was in the back, I pushed her back and lifted her Fendi dress up. The Victoria's Secret panties were soaked. She could front, but her body told the truth. I moved the panties with a little bow at the top to the side. I licked her pussy lips gently, sucked her clit, but very slowly because she loved that shit.

She grabbed my head and started grinding her pussy on my face. "Mum, oh shit, if your way of trying to… ooh shit, apologize is like this, then I accept. Fuck yes, lick right there. Mmm, yes, Yay. Do that shit, damn, boy." Milk Marie was thrashing her head back and forth. She had my dreadlocks in a vice grip. I showed no mercy. I unbuttoned my Levi's before she could catch her breath. I had dick in her, pounding her out.

"Oh shit, I feel you in my lungs, boy. Bae, chill… chill, mmm shit. Make this pussy cum, make it cum," she moaned as I jackhammered my dick in her, shaking the whole truck. This is just what I needed. I was pissed off. Pissed that Han was dead. Pissed because I had to get this money up. Pissed because I got shot. I took it all out on Milk Marie's pussy.

Once we were done, we drove in front of the mall. A few minutes later, Patron pulled up in a black Impala like Ice Cube had in *All About the Benjamins*. He didn't have any rims on it, and I thought, *my boy learnin*. I was about to get out the truck when Milk Marie grabbed my hand.

"Please, Yay, be careful. Call me when you done whatever it is you're doing." She was really serious.

"I got to get some answers and I got to get shit shaking to get this doe up. But thanks for your concern," Kissing her hand, I said, "You might want to fix your hair," getting out of the truck.

"Damn it, Yay. It's your fault, but I'm not mad. Just come back to a bitch in one piece," she said out the driver's window. As she drove off, I hopped in the car with Patron.

"What's up, big homie? What the business is?" he said, dapping me up, all teeth 14-karat gold.

"Nothing much, homie, like the nigga in *Hustle & Flow* said, 'It's hard out here for a pimp.' But yo, we got to see Shitty Smitty, Patron."

"Hell naw, man. Remember that fool sold me a pound of sour dee? I got back to the trap. It was sour, but there was no "Dee." Yuh feel me? He a con artist, dawg. I had six ounces of loud and ten ounces of some bullshit mid. Man, fuck Shitty Smitty," Patron said.

I started laughing because I remember it was last year. I saved Shitty Smitty's life because Patron was going to slump his ass. See, Shitty Smitty was the type of dude, if he didn't fuck with you or didn't know you, your ass was getting got straight like that. But Patron told Shitty Smitty it was for someone else. Therefore, Shitty Smitty took ten ounces of loud out and added midgrade. The sour dee was so potent, it took a week before certain niggas caught on. Patron was heated, but I added Shitty Smitty to the team.

His foul hustle, though dangerous, was lucrative. Shitty Smitty worked at a garage he owned. He was dark skinned with a little afro and a pot belly. But don't be fooled. Shitty Smitty had some doe niggas run him out of Detroit and he moved to Edenton, which was thirty minutes from us.

"Yo, I feel you, but I'm in a bind. I owe one-point-five million dollars to Han Che, Patron. But to pull some capers, but not where we rest at. I got some doe, but one-point-five I don't have."

"Okay, I got yuh back, but fuck we need Shitty Smitty for, homie?" he said, pulling out the mall parking lot. I was listening to Prodigy on Patron's radio, rapping about the Illuminati.

"Look, only one reason he got caught up with you because he told me he usually put all the weed in a binder. He said that's the first time anyone caught on, because he didn't mix it right. He threw it all mixed in Ziplocs. He know how to cut corners, and I got a plan."

"As usual, you the brains, but I lost a little clientele behind that weed shit," Patron said bitterly.

"That's because you know your customers really don't know. You knew and gave a few niggas a break. He sold you the pound for twenty-three hundred. You sold ounces three hundred a pop. You made forty-eight hundred, and you still smoked. You made twenty-five hundred dollars in profit. And you wonder why I'm trying to get up with Shitty Smitty?" I said, leaning back in the passenger seat.

"Damn, nigga. You a damn mathematician now? But shit, those white boys on the beach loved it though. I feel you, so we going to see Shitty Smitty," Patron said.

"No doubt, and I appreciate you having my back, homie," I said, giving him a pound with my fist.

"Shit, I'm good because of you. So, it's whatever. Damn. One-point-five million." Patron whistled. "So, how long?" he said, pulling a ready rolled blunt out of a silver case.

"I got one damn week. Yo, I know you not 'bout to light that up while we driving. You know how I am. I fucked around and sparked one in Milk Marie's Tahoe. I wasn't thinking, because she had me heated. You know I almost caught a case just because cops smelled weed in the car," I said, bobbing my head to Prodigy.

"Yo, Yay, you my nigga and all. No disrespect, but you got bigger problems. I got license, registration, and all I got is four blunts." He held up the one he had in his hand. "Including this one. I got blunt spray and the car clean," he said smiling his gold teeth.

"Oh, but I'm not clean, so I guess I need to put these in the trunk," I said, showing my Desert Eagle on my hip and my 357 in my left shoulder holster. He immediately pulled over at a rest stop.

"Yo, we going to talk to Shitty Smitty, or are we going to smoke his ass? I got my punk ass nine in the stash spot. Damn, it's that bad?" he said, popping the trunk.

"Patron, one-point-five million is what I owe." I said tossing my heaters in the trunk. Shoulder was aching but other than that I was good.

"Damn, I feel you. One-point-five million. Yeah, that's hell of a number." He fired up the blunt. "We at a rest stop, so I won't smoke this in the car." All I could do was smile.

"Now you learning. Blunt spray or not, no need to make yourself hot. People that don't smoke smell that shit," I nodded at the blunt Patron was hitting, "a mile away." He passed me the blunt. Some big white girl was getting out a trucker's truck, arguing with him.

"So, we just popping up on Shitty Smitty? What if he not down with your scheme?" Patron said, watching the big white chic thumb a ride.

I hit the blunt, realizing it was some Purple Haze. "Well," I said, enjoying the smoke numbing my shoulder, "I'll just make him an offer he can't refuse."

Fre$h

Chapter Six

Gotta Make Something Shake...

I was high as gas prices, thinking of how the fuck I was going to come up with one-point-five million. You be amazed what you can do when your back is against the wall. I had a plan. I would lose a main guy, but fuck 'em. His name was Felipe, and he only knew me as Easy. I met him in the county jail. Me and Milk Marie got drunk one night, arguing about her going to see her kids. I never really got in her business. But time went by, and she never really pushed the issue. I didn't like it.

Someone must have called the police because they were at the apartment. Shit, we opened the door talking shit to the police. We had to do forty-eight hours. I met Felipe in jail. He was in for indecent liberties with a minor. Felipe Gomez Jr. likes them R Kelly young. Really, he was a scumbag in the worst way, but this fool had a little change. He was married to a wealthy lady named Teresa Gomez, but her maiden name was Teresa Goozman. She was the daughter of internet tycoon, Joseph R. Goozman, who invested in the franchise of Arby's, then to the coffee business. Three times a day, if you watched television, you would see the ads.

Anyway, Felipe got caught cheating, drugs you name it. She even gave him alimony to get rid of him. It was half a million, I think. But in three years of that settlement word was he was fucking it up. Wild parties in Ohio where he lives in an office duplex. Word is, he lives in it. Who gives a fuck? Once a month, he copped ten keys for thirty thousand a pop and I only had to pay fifteen a key to Han, RIP, so imagine my profit. A hundred fifty thousand, no sweat, which is the same amount I invested in the thirty apartments in E-City duplex. No one really knew this. I even had two tinted window businesses in Greenville and Snow Hill. This is why I couldn't pick up and run. I maybe could pay Han Che in a few months with what I was bringing in legally through my three investments. But this nigga said a week. So, here we have a little over a thirty-minute ride, before pulling up to Shitty Smitty's garage.

He had a nice house with a few acres of land behind the garage. We pulled up, and I saw Patron get his gun from the hidden compartment under his seat. He smiled with his gold teeth. "Go see what Shitty Smitty grimy ass talking about. I got you," Patron said, kissing the nine then putting it on his lap. I just nodded and got out. I walked up to the garage. Skinny white dude was changing a tire. It was a small waiting area. I thought, *business must be good.* Beside the skinny white guy changing the tire, a pot belly black ass, oily short guy with an afro was changing the oil in a Chevy. The garage only had room for the two cars. One was low, and the other one Shitty Smitty was working on was in the air on the lift, while he was draining the oil.

"Excuse me. I want a tune-up on my car, tires rotated, oil change, and if possible, I'd like it detailed," I said in a snobbish manner.

"I'm sorry, mister, but we close in an hour. We don't detail." He never looked up from what he was doing.

"Well, what kind of shit is that?" I said until Shitty Smitty recognized who he was talking to.

"Who the hell do you think you are?" He looked up at me from under the car. "Oh shit, my man, Yay. Hey, James," he said, leaving the car he was just under. "After you finish with Cynthia's tire, finish this oil change. We done for the day." He walked up to me. "What's happening, Rick Ross

Jr., of course, I'm not talking about the rapper. What do a hardworking man owe the pleasure of your presence?"

We walked outside the garage. The smell was killing my high. "You still doing a little bit of this and a little bit of that?" I said, looking at him with greasy suspenders on. He reminded me of Cedric the Entertainer, and he always had jokes.

"Now, Yay," Shitty Smitty said pulling at his overalls with car grease on them. "I'm running an honest business, and I'm just trying to keep the bills paid."

"I think if we pull it off, you'll profit fifty thousand," I said, rotating my shoulder. I popped a painkiller. He looked at me in surprise.

"Damn, well um, fifty thousand could damn sure keep the bills paid. What you need?" Shitty Smitty said, all ears now.

"Well, I got six and a half keys. It's eighty percent pure. How far can you stretch it?" I asked.

He rubbed his chin, thinking. "Well, anything after twelve keys will be chopped to nothing. I could make you twenty, but the only thing it would past is the test. You know tube turn blue, then it's coke. But it would be weak to use. Basically crap. Why? What's up?" he said, looking towards the Impala.

"Shit if you can whip twenty keys out of six and a half, do it. But one key needs to be decent," I said, following Shitty Smitty's gaze.

"Hey, who is that you got with you in the car, Yay? You still fucking with that white girl? Know you usually roll with the ladies," he said, punching my arm playfully. On cue, Patron got out of the Impala and lit a blunt of Purple.

"Sup Shitty Smitty, wit yo slimy ass?" Patron said, leaning on the hood of the Impala with his middle finger raised.

"Oh, hell naw! If that crazy nigga a part of this, I'm out. Yay, you a hustling nigga. I give you that, but Patron pulled out the biggest gun on me I've ever seen," Shitty Smitty said mumbling, walking back towards the garage.

"Whatever, nigga. I should have made you a memory on a t-shirt, but I spared you, fool. So, you're welcome," Patron taunted Shitty Smitty, yelling back.

"Chill, dawg, I'm in a bind. Yo, Shitty, hold up, man. That shit is over with. Plus, that's the game. This is fifty thousand, you can pull it off." I turned back around towards the car. "Find someone else to whip the seven birds," I said over my shoulder.

"Okay, Yay. Okay, but you know I'm not with the violence. You know I have clean cons." Then he rubbed his chin. "I thought you said six and a half bricks?" "Did I?" I shrugged, "I might have said seven bricks, but you didn't hear me because you bullshitting," I said, tired of playing with Shitty Smitty.

"Let me hear it then," Shitty Smitty said.

"Hear what? I told you fifty large if you down," I said, walking towards Patron taking the blunt.

"No, Nino Brown. I mean, your plan to get the fifty large from this source," Shitty Smitty said, taking the blunt.

"So, you down then?" I said. Shitty Smitty was coughing his lungs up. The Purple was a beast, and he usually smoked some Reggie, which was regular midgrade.

"Yeah, I'm down. Sure didn't get it from you," Patron said, taking the blunt. I just shook my head, then started laying down the plan to Shitty Smitty.

Chapter 7

A Lick is a Lick...

Felipe called me a few days before all this bullshit happened. He even told me he might need more keys. Obviously, Felipe only had one more lump sum coming from his ex-wife. The gravy train was getting thin now. More keys? I figured if Shitty Smitty could stretch seven keys into twenty keys, then I'd only hit those I didn't know like that. In this game, no one uses their real name. Fake ID was nothing to get situated. Out of the three times I met him, Milk Marie only came once. Felipe was drooling over her, and I feel it's part of the reason he wanted the keys, just to hope to see her. But, it's not that I was a hater. I don't like Felipe, and I felt he knew it. I know one day I would move on him, so I played my part.

The best part was, in two days he was coming to Virginia Beach, which was only an hour away from me. Now I didn't have to pay for a plane ticket for me and Shitty Smitty to go to Ohio. That made me feel lucky. Patron had dropped me off at Shitty Smitty's, which is where he was working his magic with the keys I had brought back. I let Shitty Smitty keep half a hey and the work was good. Every damn key looked official. He made twenty-five keys, and told me one was still good to play in. The other twenty-four would pass a drug tester, but they would not get a damn fly high, it was chopped down so thin.

I called Felipe about 3:00 am and it never failed. This guy partied this late at forty-nine years old. As usual, the same introduction.

"Easy, my man. How's it hanging? I guess pretty good, since you're a black guy." He laughed his lame laugh.

"Where is little Mariah Carey?" Felipe said, referring to Milk Marie.

"She okay. She sends her love. Just giving you a ring. Didn't know if you needed any assistance," I said, watching Shitty Smitty Saran Wrap the keys he just whipped.

"Easy, I tell you what, bring all you got because, um, things are a bit rough and I need to make a play myself," Felipe said, sounding like he was slapping a girl on her ass while on the phone. "Just got a new piece of ass. She is a great fuck, but she is a walking vacuum cleaner. So, meet me at the Sun Dial Hotel, let's say four pm. My plane leaves at six pm, and that's one of the things my ex-wife trying to get back."

"That's fine. I know where that is, but do you have a car? Works better that way, because we both get what we want." I stood outside of Shitty Smitty's garage, watching Milk Marie pull up.

"Yeah, I have a car for yuh. And amigo, I need that young lady to be twenty years old." Then he kind of whispered in the phone, "You know I like them a little younger, but what can I say, things change."

He was referring to how many bricks he wanted. But the slick comment about liking them younger pissed me off a beat. But I laughed it off. "Sure, Vato. I'll make sure she is twenty years old." I hung up.

I got in the truck. The smell of Chanel No5, mixed with the light smell of vodka, was in the truck with Milk Marie. Milk had been drinking. I wish I knew what was up with her. I was happy Felipe was coming early. No way he was going to buy twenty keys, because he barely got the ten he usually got. I needed things to go smooth and Milk Marie wasn't focused.

"You alright, ma? You need me to get you a drink or something?" I said, concerned.

"No, Yay, I brought the bottle of Avion to drink with you. I know it's your favorite. I had a little vodka and tonic before I left," she said, pulling out of Shitty Smitty's driveway. "I got everything you asked for, but I'm telling you, Yay, I don't want to go around Felipe's ass. Fool always trying to hug me and feel my ass. Dude is a real clown. Why do you deal with him?"

"Because he spends, but I got a feeling I won't be seeing him anymore. I think we will part ways by tomorrow," I said, poppin the bottle of Avion. Now let's go to the Boardwalk. We will be in VA in an hour," I said, leaning back for the ride.

"Why you going so early? I thought you had to see Felipe like four pm? It's almost four am," she said, but she kept driving towards VA. She had jeans on with a few rips in them, some KD sneakers that matched a Cardi shirt. Yeah, Milk Marie had some swag.

"Because, baby," rotating my right shoulder while sippin the Avion tequila, "the early bird catches the worm." I said, leaning back in my seat, putting in a Mobb Deep CD called *Murder Muzik*. The song, "We Should Spread Love Not War" came on with horns blaring. "Because you won't feel safe coming out your krib, knowing that we got beef." I thought what I always know. *Ain't no love, just war.* I was playing mental warfare. Fuck it! A lick is a lick.

Fre$h

Chapter 8

It Is What It Is...

Boardwalk Inn was nice, but not as nice as the Sun Dial Hotel, but from my room I could see the Sun Dial Hotel. We were pretty much on the strip. It wasn't freezing cold, more of a chill. Traffic was back up in front of the McDonald's. People still rode bicycles and walked across the boardwalk with bikinis on. Some young guys with wet suits on were on their way to the beach. I loved Virginia Beach, especially the Strip. It was where plays and hustles were made.

See, from a regular point of view, this is what you saw, parents with kids and people from out of town. The Strip had clubs, vapor clubs, souvenir shops, other hotels, etc., all up and down. There was even a carnival, if you walked further down the beach. Great atmosphere if you were watching from a regular point of view. But what I saw when I turned on my tunnel vision was the guy on the corner with a bald head selling pot. I saw a white guy with a suit and tie on talking to a pretty white female in a sundress. The guy in the suit nodded to the muscular guy, the muscular guy held up one finger, and the guy with the suit went to the hotel with the girl in the sundress.

I had an hour and a half before me and Shitty Smitty had to meet Felipe. It was about 2:30 pm. Patron and Shitty Smitty were in a room beside me, getting ready. Milk Marie had sexed me last night, but she kept saying she was sorry after.

"Look, if it's about the last few days you were gone, don't sweat it. I know what it is with us. You good," I said last night, rolling over in bed.

"What if I wanted to be more than what we are? What if I never said the first night I wanted to pretend you were mine?" she said, pushing her hair out of her face. "I know you're different. It's my fault. But is there any way I can change it?" she said, rolling me over.

"Let's talk about it tomorrow. Okay?" I said, needing some sleep. I had been up all day, keeping Patron and Shitty Smitty from arguing. They were finally getting along. I stayed up with Shitty Smitty to make the bricks. I sexed Milk Marie and that had me beat. She laid on my chest and fell asleep. Now it was time to see if Shitty Smitty could pull off this con.

I had an all-black Rastafarian crown covering my dreads. Dark gray Armani suit with a black tie and black wing-tipped Gucci shoes, and Gucci shades—dark black with the Gucci logo in the middle of the shades, completed my attire. I threw back two painkillers. My shoulder was hurting like hell. I needed to eat, but the Avion was numbing me.

Milk Marie was out of the shower and dressed in a gray Chanel pantsuit with Chanel frames and black Chanel heels. We looked at each other in the mirror. We did look like a nice couple. She even took a selfie to memorialize the moment. I had everything Milk Marie brought with her from the apartment. Her fake ID was Maria Sanchez. Mine was Eric Roberts. Shitty Smitty was Thomas Gage. After today, none of the IDs would be worth a damn. I looked through my binoculars and the muscular guy was still standing there. I spoke into my cufflink. "Yo, Patron, everything good in there?" I asked, releasing the button.

"Yeah, my dude. Everything, everything... This nigga going from *Meet the Browns* to Gerald Levert." Patron laughed, "Yo, Yay, where you get this spy shit from? You got another life or something? Are you some lost relative of

Shaft or something? This shit is dope. I got it stuck on my ear like an earring," Patron said in the two-way receiver.

"I told you I had a retired arms dealer who has all kinds of shit. How is the sniper rifle?" I said, watching Milk Marie pour herself some Avion.

"Man, this shit high tech. I got it all assembled. So, after this is over with, I can keep this shit?" Patron said.

The plan was Patron watched our backs until we were back on the highway. Milk Marie was on standby in the Tahoe for a quick getaway, if needed. From our rooms, you could see the Sun Dial. There was a restaurant and Felipe liked sitting by the window. The garage could be seen as well. We were to park in garage B-42. The car we needed was parked in B-43. Patron had been in the military for a short while, but he would have a problem. He fucked his commander's wife. Lucky to just get discharged. He could still hit an apple from a thousand feet. Guess the Marines taught him something, "Hoorah."

Anyway, looking out my binoculars again, the girl in the sundress came out to meet the muscle guy. He held up one finger to the guy in the suit. I knew that meant one hour had gone by.

"Okay, places, gentlemen. And yes, Patron, we get out of this, you can have the sniper rifle." Milk Marie gave me a kiss and walked out the door. I met up with Shitty Smitty downstairs. I had to admit he did look like Gerald Levert. He had a Camry with fake tags, and it was already parked in B-42.

We were crossing one of the boardwalks. It was taking us across to the McDonald's, next door was the parking garage. Then the Sun Dial Hotel would be standing there with a big restaurant on the bottom floor. Patron could see everything, because the scope of the sniper rifle was powerful enough.

Patron could adjust the dial and look in the restaurant so close, he would be able to see the food on the diner's plates. Plus, if anything got out of control, we had that edge.

Polo was my boy, but Patron was my dawg. I was ready to make the switch, then get ghost. Once across the street, we walked to the garage. I glanced at Shitty Smitty, "You good, man?" I asked. He only nodded at me. He must have been nervous. Hell, I was nervous too, but I could tell Shitty Smitty liked the rush. I was counting on him because he was going to pose as my boss figure. If I was alone, he might want to chitchat. Maybe order a few rounds. I was in a bit of a rush.

"Okay, I've been around this prick, so let me just run through it. Once you follow my lead, we should fall in play." We walked inside the restaurant. "How do we look up there?" I said into my cufflink.

"Good and crystal clear. I'm looking at one of the slime balls now. Bald spot looks like a fake Tony Montana," Patron said, referring to the *Scarface* gangsta flick.

"Okay. Just be my eyes. We go silent from here," I said getting to a big table. Once I got to the table, I noticed there were not too many other people in the room besides us. Felipe was getting up to greet me. Some girl, who looked at least fifteen, was dressed all up and rubbing her nose. This must have been the vacuum Felipe spoke of. There was one guy seated at a booth nursing a beer. There was another guy seated opposite him doing the same. They both had on shades. As far as I could tell, neither man ever touched the beer. I was getting a bit worried. I looked around the restaurant. It was damn near deserted.

"Yayo, what's up, my friend? How's it hanging, black man, huh?" He laughed, hugging me.

"Hiyuh doing, Felipe? This is Mr. Gage, who I work for," I said, nodding at Shitty Smitty.

"Ah, yes." He shook Shitty's hand. "Please, both of you, sit. This is Isabella," he said, settling down. She was very pretty but looked like she should be in school. This was one of the many reasons I didn't like this guy.

She played with her nose but said, "Hi," to us. Then she licked her lips at me. I ignored her, and I asked the waiter for water. After I got my water, Shitty spoke up.

"Sorry if you had plans to have dinner, but I have to get to Las Vegas." He plucked at invisible lint on his chocolate brown Hilfiger suit. He had Stacy Adams on, with a burgundy bow tie and a burgundy handkerchief in the left breast top pocket. He had cut his fro down to a nice Caesar. He looked like an expensive, black lawyer.

"Right you are, Mr. Gage." Speak of the devil. Just then some guy in a cheap suit came up and whispered to Felipe. Then he stepped to the side. "Mr. Gage and Easy, let's go to the parking garage so you can get to Vegas." Felipe got up, leading the way. The guy that brought the message stayed with Isabella, but both obvious bodyguards fell in line with us.

The air was getting stale in the parking lot of car tires and motor oil. We walked to 52 and 53. Felipe tapped on 52 and once the garage door came up, it was dark inside. Felipe stepped inside. I hesitated. Felipe peeped his head back out, "Don't be shy," he said, waving us in. Once the bodyguards came up behind us, the garage door shut. I was trying not to panic. I was hoping Shitty Smitty was cool. This was not a part of the plan.

Out-of-the-blue in the dark, Shitty Smitty said, "Damn, it's dark as hell in here." Someone snickered, and then everyone started to laugh. That moment, the interior lights came on. Some big ass Cuban, looking like the Rock, was in a gray suit and purple shirt. His shoes looked expensive. Then it clicked in my head. This was Felipe's older brother, Esteban. Now I know why he was getting the ten keys. It was his brother, not him. This was the biggest deal, and he was exposing it by being present like this. The Camry was in the garage. Someone must have moved it. The restaurant crap was a diversion. Mr. Gage took over and put on for the room. He pressed a button on some key he had. It popped the trunk open.

"Show me yours and I'll show you mine, big guy," Shitty Smitty said, with not a quiver in his voice.

"There is four hundred fifty thousand in a Mitsubishi Galant in the garage beside us. Ten keys paid for, and half the rest will come in a week. I hope this is ok," Esteban said with a slick grin.

Sorry ass was taking us for a ride, and I thought it was ironic. I mean, Esteban was shorting me on half a brick. No talk beforehand at all. If this had been any other time, I would have debated. Due to the present issue, I let it slide. Esteban was going through the trunk. Mr. Gage tossed him the button that looked like a key chain. One of the bodyguards tossed some keys to me. We were about to walk out. Esteban was pulling the carpet part back in the trunk. The keys were stacked neatly where there was no spare tire. Esteban pulled out a big fucking Rambo knife.

"Excuse me, Mr. Gage," Esteban said, stopping everyone. Esteban licked the knife and stabbed a hole in the key on top. I almost shit myself. Was it the key Shitty Smitty had left bare?

Esteban pulled the knife out and snorted damn near everything on the knife. He then licked it again while walking up to us. He paused, snorted to clear his nose a few times, then stuck out his hand to Shitty Smitty. He said, "Good to finally meet you, Mr. Gage."

Fre$h

Chapter 9

Clean Up as You Go...

I only pulled over once because Shitty Smitty was hyperventilating. "Holy shit! Holy shit! We did it! That big dude was scary as fuck." He was slapping me on the arms. "Yayo, you crazy mothafucka! You did it," Shitty Smitty said, rolling his window down to get some air.

We were on our way to a chop shop in Chesapeake. Had to get rid of this car. While Shitty Smitty was hyperventilating, I pulled over. I checked the trunk. Under a black tarp was ten-thousand-dollar stacks neatly in the trunk that added up to four hundred and fifty thousand dollars. Holy shit! Then I realized... What the hell I was celebrating for? I had to give this money to Han Che. But hell, it should buy me time. Patron said he would link back up. I promised to break him off. He was ready to stash the sniper rifle.

"Yo, I love this 007 shit," Patron said, before hanging up leaving back to Moyock area.

Milk Marie caught up with us at the chop shop. She called me and said, "Yay, you're fucking crazy. But I'm glad you got that damn pedophile," she said on the phone.

I only got two thousand for the Mitsubishi, but I gave it to Milk Marie. I was going to drive the burgundy Chevy Caprice I bought from Derek at the chop shop. I told him I needed some wheels. I still had Shirley, but I didn't really drive it. I was going to get my BMW out the shop, but it was on ice. I liked the Chevy Caprice. It was not something I'd usually drive. So, he gave me a good deal. I let Shitty Smitty drive it home. Told him I'd get it later, and with his well-earned fifty thousand in the trunk, he was set.

We both went into a rest area off the highway and changed clothes. Jordans, Levi's and a long-sleeved black shirt, my dreads still in a ponytail, black G-shock watch and I was ready. Two duffel bags were loaded in the Tahoe. Plus, I had Shitty Smitty's clothes and fake IDs. He went his way in my Caprice, and Milk Marie and I pulled off in the opposite direction. Once we were back in the city of Moyock, I called everyone to touch base and make sure everyone made it to their destinations safely. I then told Milk Marie to pull up at this rundown gas station, to a metal dumpster in the back. We drove up to it, I put all our fake IDs in the dumpster, along with the clothes Shitty Smitty and I had worn.

I reached under the seat to get the paper bag that had lighter fluid in it. I splashed lighter fluid on everything in the dumpster and lit a whole book of matches to toss on top of it. I walked away from the fire blazing inside the dumpster, and I jumped back inside the Tahoe. Milk Marie drove off as I called Boost to change my number.

I texted my new number to Milk, Shitty and Patron. I went to Western Union and had a few grand sent to my aunt in Woodbridge, VA. Milk Marie did it in her name. I never liked my name on anything. Only thing that had my government was the part ownership with two others who owned the E-City duplex I lived in, and only one of the tinted window shops. The one in Snow Hill was done over a handshake.

Something hit me though, and that was I had a little over four hundred thousand dollars. I had two hundred fifty thousand of my own. I could just leave. Maybe go to Silverdale, Washington. I had a shorty I knew named Sandra Klark. She had a thick body like Khloe Kardashian. Sandra invested in two furniture chains. Now it's at five and counting. A few postcards she sent, it looked like it was nice there. Then I thought about Han getting shot. I started punching the dashboard.

"Yay, calm down, baby. What is it?" Milk Marie said, still driving. I calmed down and leaned back. I took a deep breath.

"Sorry about your truck. I'm good. It's just..." I was rubbing my forehead. "I cannot believe Han is dead. This shit is pissing me off. Someone did this, and I want to know who," I said as we pulled up to the apartment. I sat and thought for a minute. Maybe I could get some answers from the man himself. I scrolled through my phone, and Han Che's name was in the contacts. Had it been there before? So much was going on. I still didn't even know where the phone came from. I was assuming Larry, since he had clothes for me as well. Didn't have time to bother with that now. I pressed send on the contact.

"Yes," Han Che said.

"I have something for you," I replied.

"Something doesn't sound like all. What exactly is something, Yay?" Han Che said in his laidback tone.

"I have four hundred thousand and I'm getting up as much as possible to right this wrong." I said.

"Impressive. No wonder my son liked you. You know where Garage 5 is?" Then the phone hung up. I needed to go alone, but Han Che knew of Milk Marie. Plus, Shitty Smitty had my Caprice. I called the impound, sent Patron to get it, and put it on ice. Then I told Milk Marie my destination.

On the ride to the Toyota dealership, I thought of growing up with Patron, looking like B.G. from the Hot Boys. We were close at a young age. So close, in fact, that a Puerto Rican lady named Mrs. Jefferson and her black husband, Jeremy Jefferson, adopted us, thinking we were brothers. We grew up in Richmond, VA. We ended up in Virginia Beach.

My aunt, Nancy Baxter, found me when I was sixteen and Patron fourteen. My mother and father were killed in a car accident when I was three. I had been left with the babysitter, and I guess that is how I ended up in the system. Luckily, my aunt stayed in Virginia Beach near Military Highway. So, I wasn't too far from Patron.

I was trying to adjust because I didn't really know my aunt. She had a few pictures of my mom, but she did not have any of my dad. We watched scary movies. She had a husband, but he had passed away before she found me. Aunt Nancy signed me up for the Boys & Girls Club. Patron had gotten into some trouble, so he could not go sometimes. I still kept in touch with the Jeffersons.

I was at the Boys & Girls Club standing outside. From the area where the bleachers sat, I caught the distinct smell of pot. I walked over to find this Chinese kid smoking a joint underneath the bleachers. He had on jeans, Vans, and a Quicksilver shirt. His hat was on backwards, and his hair was falling out of the back snap.

"Hey, yo, don't just stare, homeboy. You trying to hit this, then come under here," Han said, looking around.

"Shit smell good," I said, sitting beside him Indian style.

"I'm Han," he said, passing the joint, "And this is my girlfriend, Mary Jane."

"My friends call me Yay. Are you from Virginia, Han?" I said, hitting the joint twice then passing it back.

"No. I'm from Compton, CA. Moved here two years ago when my mom passed. I've never went in," Han said.

"What? You've never went in? Got some girls in there. There is a light-skinned girl named Stephanie with a big ole booty. She mine. So, you can have the others," I said, dusting myself off. But Han was still sitting there. "Yo, Han,

get your ass up. Let's go play some ping pong," I said, watching him get up.

"I may be Chinese, but that don't mean I know how to play ping pong," he said, but in a joking way.

"Come on. You know what I mean."

We went inside and got into a heated foosball match. Stephanie and her friend, Sasha, cheered us on. Sasha had her eyes on Han the whole time. Han jumped on his tippy toes, spun the bar with the men on it, and BANG, the ball went in the goal. We won.

Me and Han were celebrating when this big assed kid named Dirty started calling us cheaters. Dirty's nickname fit him well. He was dirty looking, but he was bigger than any of the other kids.

"Hey, man, we got rules about spinning the bar like that. So, we have to play again," Dirty said, changing the point.

All games go to ten and the game was intense because it was nine to nine before Han's spin move shot the ball and won the game. Little JJ, Dirty's partner, was already walking away.

"Yo, they won, Dirty. I'm going to the gym, man," Little JJ said, turning towards the water fountain.

"Hell no, man, these Rush Hour looking niggas going to play again, and it's point-point, our ball," Dirty said, adjusting the foosball table.

"Look, homie, we won. So, that's it. Now this is the third game, and you was even jerking the table. But we still beat you." Han turned to me and said, "I need some fresh air. You coming?"

Before I could respond, Dirty got all in Han's face. "I said," Dirty spoke while gritting his teeth, "We play again."

Han looked at me, sighed, and as if it was a movie, punched Dirty in the nuts. At the same time, everybody yelled, *"Oooouuuu!"* Then, Han chopped Dirty in the throat, and did a roundhouse kick, making contact with Dirty's face. This sent Dirty to the floor where he was writhing in pain, with one hand on his nuts and the other on his throat.

Han casually walked to the exit door. He turned his hat back to its backwards position, and he yelled, "Yo, Yay, you coming, homie?" I was too busy looking at Dirty on the floor moaning in pain.

Stephanie and Sasha came outside with us. We smoked another joint together. Sasha kissed Han on the cheek. Then she and Stephanie left together. I was watching Han light up another blunt. He felt me staring at him.

"What's up, Yay? Something on my face?" he asked with a smirk.

Taking the blunt, I said, "Fool, why you didn't tell 'em you knew karate?" still laughing from what Han had done to Dirty.

"Homie, I said I didn't play ping pong. I never said shit about Kung Fu." We were both cracking up under the bleachers. Ever since that day, we were tight.

Once Milk Marie and I pulled up at the Toyota dealership, I told Milk Marie to go to the back and pull up at Garage 5. She seemed a little nervous. So, I said, "Yo, Milk, I'm just going to talk to Han Che for a second. You okay?" I turned the music down a little.

"I'm good, Yay. It's just Han Che give me the creeps and his bodyguards too," Milk Marie said, pushing her hair out the way of her shoulders.

Once we pulled up to Garage 5, the garage door started to lift up. I told Milk Marie to drive on in. As the door closed behind us, lights came on illuminating the room. The garage was roomy enough for the Tahoe. To my right was a platform, with stairs leading off into a hallway. Both bodyguards Milk Marie had just been talking about were posted up waiting. One had long, dark hair in a ponytail. He always kept shades on day and night. I was sure he slept in them. He looked like the dude Bolo from all the Van Damme movies, but he always made me feel I was in no danger. He would always nod at me and say, "Yayo Sun, it's a pleasure."

I got out the truck and went to the back. The other big ass Chinese dude was like the other guy's twin. He had a dragon tattooed on the side of his bald head though. He never said anything. He just grunted and nodded. Wang was his name. Fujj was the bald headed one with the dragon tattoo. Wang walked to the back on the truck.

"Yayo Sun, it's always a pleasure. Of course, you know I must frisk you," Wang said.

Once done, he told me I would get my Desert Eagle back when my business with Han Che had concluded. Wang and Fujj had the duffel bags. As I walked up the steps, Wang said, "Yayo Sun." When I looked back at him, he said "When all of this is figured out, I will be there to finish things. So, I pray this wrong will be righted," he said, duffel bag on his huge shoulder. All I could do was nod my head.

Once down the hallway, I came to a huge office. There were monitors on one side of the wall. Han Che was smoking a hand-rolled Cuban. Pictures of Han were up. Some of back home, I assumed, pictures of Han Che with Suge Knight at an L.A. Clippers game. Some with other celebrities like Jackie Chan.

Shit, he even had a picture with him and Tupac. I was in awe, because there was a lot about Han Che I still didn't know. There was an expensive looking vase with candles around it. I knew it was Han, and I was brought back to reality. Han Che was watching me as he walked from behind a huge mahogany desk. Two big statues of Samurai warriors were on each side. There was a big onyx table with two black couches opposite both sides.

The Cuban smelled good, and the aroma was closer. Han Che was behind me. I looked at the picture of Tupac. Han Che gestured to one of the black couches and said, "I remember my younger days. He was on the video set of 'California Love.' For a guy from a very poor family, he rose up and became rich. But see, Yayo, the key is you have to keep your worlds very, very separated. He was, to your people, the next Malcolm X. Sadly, he didn't shake his demons in time," Han Che said, pouring me as well as himself, a drink. Once again, the bottle of Louis XIII cognac was in his hand.

I thought back to Tiger Woods' restaurant. I was sipping on a small glass of liquor worth about two grand per shot. Some people made that in a month, working daily. I was sipping on somebody's paycheck, and I suddenly knew I never ever wanted to be broke again.

This is why I couldn't run or try to hide. Han getting killed had nothing to do with me. But I had made a decent amount of money in the game. Fuck being shook and looking over my shoulder. I would pay the debt best way I knew how—the streets. But no matter what, I wanted to smoke the fools who tried to take me with Han.

As Han Che was speaking about Tupac, Wang came in to report what was in the two duffel bags.

"It's four hundred thousand on the head, Han Che." He nodded to Han Che, then looked at me with a smirk and walked out.

Han Che was draped in a silk green and tan Versace shirt with all-white Versace slacks. The black Versace loafers with the gold buckle set off the Versace glasses. I've seen

Puffy and Biggie rock it on TV, but this nigga was wearing it as if it was pajamas.

"Looks like you've been busy boy. But I still have a million owed to me. For other people, this would be how Americans say impossible." Han Che sipped his expensive drink and looked at me dead in the eyes. "But we are in a league of gentlemen that make the impossible possible. I know the issue in the car bothered you. And, yes, I know you and Han were close. So, I'm asking you, now that you've put something on the bill—are you sure, Yayo, you know nothing about receiving the hundred bricks my son claims he gave you?" He leaned back on the couch, sipping and rubbing his goatee.

"Come on, Han Che," I said, rotating my right shoulder, still aching. "I just stepped up twenty-five of them thangs a few months ago. There is no way a hundred bricks came to me and Han never told me." I took the whole shot. "I was only supposed to get twenty-five period at a key." I realized I was rolling a blunt and then didn't know if Han Che would let me spark it. He just nodded at me nonchalantly.

"You have your needs," he held up the expensive bottle, "and I have mine," he said as he poured himself another glass.

I sparked the blunt, and I felt a lot better. Fuck being scared. It was time to man up.

"Look, Han Che, I paid your son two hundred thousand up front, then a hundred seventy-five once I got it. I'm losing almost a quarter of a million. And I owe you a million that I have no knowledge of." I said in frustration, "I'm telling you. I catch one nigga talking Russian, I'm killing his ass," inhaling the sour diesel I rolled.

For the first time since this whole damn ordeal went down, Han Che's eyes showed concern as well as anger.

"How do you know any Russian?" he asked me a bit too calmly.

"Han Che, I don't know any damn people that are Russian. I shot one of the masked guys in the ass. Right cheek, I think. Another guy was helping him limp away. I passed out soon after, but before I passed out, I heard him speak Russian. It sounded like he was cursing or something," I said finishing my blunt and crushing it in the ashtray. "Look, Han Che, I always met Han in the same spot for the last year. No problems. All of a sudden, we get ambushed." I was shaking my head confused.

"What about Polo? You know he wants to be like you. I mean, you know the saying—friends close and enemies closer and all of that," Han Che replied, lighting another Cuban.

"Naw, Polo was the one that started shooting at them fools. Plus, only me and Han knew about the meet. Milk Marie was driving. Polo was in the backseat. I waited till the last minute to tell Milk Marie I had to link up with Han," I said, feeling the liquor numb my shoulder.

"You're sure you heard one of the guys speak Russian?" Han Che seemed alert now and paying attention.

"Honestly, I think both them motherfuckers were talking Russian. Because now that I think on it, the guy I shot in the ass was cursing in Russian. Then another guy helped him limp away, speaking Russian. I feel like he was trying to tell him to hurry or something," I replied.

I heard Han Che yell for Wang and once he came in, he was telling Wang something as fast as hell in Chinese. He looked at me, then Han Che, and took off to do whatever Han Che had said.

74

"Yo, Han Che, is there something I need to know? Because I don't like being in the blind. Also, I need more time to come up with a million," I said standing to leave.

"First of all, I know you're smart. I admire you. I wanted Han to have the ability you have to invest and watch the money work for you. But my business is none of yours. The debt needs to be paid, but I will give you another week. I'm sorry, Yayo, but the last contact from my son said you were to receive the hundred bricks. Until I learn more than that, that's all I have to go on. But I agree with you on one thing that puzzles me," Han Che said, walking me to the garage area from his office.

"What's that, Han Che?" I said, with Fujj giving me back two empty duffel bags, then disappearing in another direction on an errand from Han Che.

"If no one but you and Han knew to meet at this particular place, then how did someone get that info?" he said, stopping at the door.

"Don't forget knowing what we were meeting for," I reminded him.

"Is that Milk Marie in the truck?" Han Che said.

"Yeah. My BMW was at the impound so she been driving me a little," I said, taking the last shot and handing the glass back to Han Che.

"I don't think she is what you need in a female. She fucks you, sucks you, and knows you're financially secure. But can you honestly say you trust her?" Han said, giving me advice. I mean, we weren't girlfriend and boyfriend. To be honest, I knew I didn't trust Milk Marie. I trusted what I knew. I took Han Che's advice and kept note of what he was saying.

"You remember that girl Sasha had Han ass open. The one with the big ole booty. Remember?" Han Che reminded me.

"Yeah, we knew her and Stephanie since the Boys Club days," I said, reminiscing on the past.

"Sasha tried to throw you some pussy, but you told Han. He didn't believe you. I mean, you two were thick as thieves. I didn't like Patron back then, but he grew on me. Anyway, for two weeks you two didn't talk."

"Yeah, I remember the slut felt guilty and finally told the truth," I said, remembering.

"What I am saying is don't forget to be true to who you are. Do you know why I never ever liked apples?" Han Che said grinning.

I laughed, remembering. "Yeah, you said Eve started the art of disloyalty, and the apple was a symbol of her disloyalty to not just God, but Adam as well," I said.

"That hoe was smooth talked by a snake. So, again, she brought back to Adam what she learned. These females now can't be trusted. Just saying," Han said, patting me on the back. "You know he loved you, Yay. Be safe out there and know I got an eye on you."

I got in the truck and threw the duffel bags in the back. As the garage door opened and we left, Milk Marie was looking at me. Once we were at a stoplight, she said, "So, what did Han Che say? Do he know who killed Han and damn near got you as well?" Milk Marie said to me as the light turned green. I did remember after we graduated, Sasha tried to give me some. Han was pissed, but he knew I wasn't a grimy nigga. I sat back and thought a lot about what Han Che had said.

"Um, hello, Yay. I'm talking to you, boo," she said, rubbing my leg. I've had my share of chics, but I was never serious with anyone. I was practically an orphan, and I had one aunt that barely had any other relatives. I didn't know what it was like to have a mother or a father.

Han lost his mom and didn't truly seem as close as he should be to his father. My phone had buzzed me out of my thoughts. I forgot I put it on vibrate when I was talking to Han Che. It was Polo. I texted back, "Call you in a minute." I was still in deep thought, *what's in the dark always comes to the light*. I felt Milk Marie's hands feeling on my thigh. She was telling me Wang had given her my gun. It was in a stash spot I had built in the Tahoe.

"Boo, if you're not going to talk to me, then when we get to the apartment, I'll just suck it out of you," she said, licking her lips.

Any other time, it would have turned me on. But my response was, "I'm never going to eat apples ever again," I said, gazing out the window. Milk Marie just shook her head and kept driving.

I hoped Polo had something useful to tell me. Why he was trying to get me to bounce, I couldn't understand. I mean, okay, I owed a powerful member of the Chinese cartel now a cool million. I had his son die in my arms. On top of that, a hundred bricks were taken that I never knew were for me. I mean, I could run, but where was the honor in that? I called Polo.

"What's up, gee? Tell me something good," I said, listening to Milk Marie sing along to Miley Cyrus and Juicy J's song, "Jays on My Feet."

"Okay. Try this. Some white boys with weird accents putting on the airwaves they got that lush scale," Polo said. "My man Laylow said they in a beach house in the city of Corolla."

This had to be them. I was all ears. It had to be them. I needed to ask more questions.

"Okay. What kind of accents we talking about? People are from everywhere on the beach. Po, these fools might just be tossing a few punk ass ounces."

"Um no, nigga, because Laylow asked them if they had baby birds flying and they said they had birds for days. But told Laylow to hurry, because in a few days, they were leaving town," Polo said.

"Okay. Let me know when you want to meet up. This might be them," I said, sitting up, now wide awake.

"Come through Moyock in an hour. Oh, and Laylow said one sounded like the Russian from the movie *Rocky*," Polo said.

"Say no more. See you in an hour," I said, thinking only of revenge.

Chapter 10

All in Due Time...

Well, Milk Marie was pissed off, but what was new about that? I told her instead of driving home, to take me to Shitty Smitty's house. Edenton was a twenty-minute ride. I'd be in Moyock in about thirty minutes. I phoned Shitty and told him I was coming for my car. His ass told me he had no plans of going anywhere. He was still too paranoid to leave the house. I told him to take the family on a vacation, but Shitty was already plotting another scheme.

I knew he was in the slum game. He asked me how much jewelry I had. I told him plenty, even though I had a long Figaro chain with a gold frame down to my stomach. It was a black and white picture I loved of my mother. I always kept it tucked in, mostly. But it was all I rocked. Patron used to get on me when we would go out. But that's why I got every tooth in my mouth dipped in twenty-four-karat gold, because I talked money. Everyone always said I looked like Ace Hood, but I never it paid it no mind. He was one of my favorite rappers, and he always motivated the art of the hustle.

Milk Marie pulled up to drop me off. Her face was twisted like she was upset but trying not to be. As I got out, I was about to light up the Purple I rolled.

"Yay, I don't know why I feel distance between us. I never tried or intended to hurt you. We were both mad," she said, looking at me with her shades off.

"You didn't hurt me, first of all. You opened my eyes wider to what I already knew," I said lightly but bluntly, shutting the door to the trunk.

"Oh, and what's that, Yay?" she said with attitude, looking through the passenger window.

"That giving someone or allowing someone to have all of you is dangerous, if that person isn't ready. Yes, I'm different. I got comfortable and you needed a break," I said, blowing out purple smoke.

"Yay, it wasn't like that, okay? We were something without a title and without words. I didn't know if you could turn me into..." she said, looking for the words.

"A girlfriend," I said, which was true. We had been in the apartment for two weeks fucking, laying up, watching TV, and screwing in every room. I had brought up taking her to see her kids, and she flipped. See I finally understood something that made me change how I looked at Milk Marie.

To me, she favored the chic Kat Stacks to the "T." They had the same nose, but she was a fool in the sheets. But once I got to know her, it dawned on me that she had been just running around fucking at one point, getting pregnant with an ex-husband. Black of course, two kids. Instead of leaving him, she had two kids on him. He finally left her, but her mom had all the boys.

She had five in all, and the last sperm donor took care of his kid. But I realized one thing. Milk Marie was a hoe, and you cannot turn a hoe into a housewife. As I got to know her, I now realized why her mom had the kids and barely said two words to her.

Her own brother would not acknowledge her, even in public. One day I saw him and asked him why he treated Milk Marie that way. He, his name was Matthew, said, "Man, my sister ain't shit. She lives for the moment."

You see, she had kids because she was fucking different guys. She didn't want to deal with the responsibility of kids, but still kept fucking unprotected. Before I met her, she had some shit put in her pussy not to have kids. Dick was her drug and at a young age, she was misguided. But anyway, she was having a great time. I guessed I ruined it by reminding her of her responsibilities. She was gone for days, and that was that. I never tripped. I mean, for what? I feel she was used to niggas trying to lock her down. Well, not Yayo. I chase money.

"Look, I'll holla. We still good, because I got to roll," I said, hopping in the Caprice. Keys in the ignition, windows were already tinted, tires looked good—no rims. Less attention is what I needed. Milk Marie stared at me, wiped at her eyes, and drove off. I only seen her cry once as she told me of how her stepfather had molested her. Everybody got a story to tell.

I hit the highway. The tags were good, and I told my dude at the chop shop I would just keep it in the name it was already in. I'd switch it later. I was messing with my phone downloading music. The car had an auxiliary cord. I was bumping the Ace Hood song all the way to meet Polo. "Same old shit just a different day/Gotta get this money each and every way/Momma need a house/Kids need some shoes/Times getting hard/Guess what I'm gone do/Hustle, hustle, hustle/Hard close mouth don't get fed on this boulevard"

Laylow had two-bedroom house three miles from where these fools ambushed us. I saw a Ninja bike in the yard, and a gold Camry with twenty-inch reflector rims on it. I thought the rims would look nice on my Caprice. Maybe after this mess was cleared up. As I pulled up, Laylow was at the door waving me inside. I turned the car off and went inside.

Laylow's pad was laced with all kinds of fly shit. Fly stolen shit, of course. Laylow had game, I'm telling you. He told me one time in Catholic school he lived with his aunt.

He convinced a nun to show him she had panties on. He was kicked out of the school and finished in public school. He reminded you of Smokey from the movie *Friday*. He was the nigga's twin in real life.

Once I walked inside, he dapped me up playfully. "My nigga, Yayo. What's happening, dude? Glad to see you still with us, homie. Polo spoke to me and told me to keep on the lookout," he said, sitting in a La-Z-Boy. Polo was in the kitchen making a peanut butter and jelly sandwich.

"Aye, nigga, why you always come over here eating up my shit? Better get Tawana to heat up that stove," Laylow said from the living room. Polo came in, smacking on the sandwich.

"For one, I'm gone before the sun come up and for two, I like eating up your shit. Now tell Yay what you told me," Polo said, sitting down on a red-colored velvet couch. I was sitting on the other end of the couch. Gave Polo a pound by bumping fists, watching him eat two sandwiches back-to-back.

"Okay. This is what it is," Laylow said, putting down the controls to the game system of the fifty-inch flat screen. Laylow loved stolen stuff. He has some little niggas in Ahoskie rip off Walmart, GameStop, and even break in Roses. Clean it out, and Laylow would fence all the goods in VA, Raleigh, or online. Spread the good around. Sometimes even cars, because he had an uncle who worked for the DMV. He could steal your all-white Benz and in two weeks, it would be black with a different VIN number. Everything about it would be legit. No doubt, the Camry was probably switched.

"You know I be on the beach fencing certain shit or trying to get up in one of these pretty beach houses. So, I'm going down the boardwalk, about to leave. My man, Jason, stops me," Laylow said, while rolling a blunt of sour diesel.

"Jason from Suffolk? He live on the strip now?" Polo said, wiping his hand on a napkin.

"I don't know if he moved, but Jason always plugged in to dope. He tell me some dudes with accents got bricks uncut. Jason said they got birds for days," Laylow said, passing the blunt to Polo.

"So, where the fools at? Seems you only talk to this Jason dude. You never saw the white dudes with the accents? How did they sound?" I said, taking the blunt from Polo.

"Look, one of the niggas sound like the Russian off the movie *Rocky*. You know? The dude that killed Apollo Creed and he says, in the deep voice like the Russian from the movie, 'If he dies, he dies,'" Laylow said, cracking up. "But, yo, it's on you, homie. They in a beach house in Corolla. Not only that. You know Amanda that work at the Surfboard Shop?" Laylow said to me.

"Good Pussy? You mean Amanda 'Good Pussy' Sanders? Hell yeah, I know her. She a straight powder head," I said, passing Laylow the blunt.

"Shit, Amanda got some good pussy though," Polo said. All three of us in unison were shaking our heads. Then we all laughed, realizing we'd all hit it.

"So, what's the move, Yay? You been looking for these clowns. It got to be them because they stick out like a sore thumb," Laylow said. I looked at Polo.

"Whatever you want to do, I'm with it. Them fools need to get got. But I'm trying to see if there is a payday in it. I'm not going to lie," Polo said.

"Man, say no more. If I get to kill these niggas and get the work back to Han Che, man, it's on," I said, putting my Desert Eagle in my left shoulder holster.

We all talked of what we were going to do and how we were going to do it. I told Laylow to make sure he got up with good pussy Amanda, because tomorrow night these niggas were dead!

I had finished talking to Polo and Laylow about how to approach tomorrow night's events. Polo left on his bike because Tawana was blowing him up. Laylow was going to the beach to get up with Amanda Sanders. I was in the Caprice putting some Kevin Gates in my phone when someone pulled up in a red Beamer.

A girl got out of the red Beamer. She was rocking Jimmy Choo stilettoes, with the little purse to match. I peeped, and her dress was a mixture of green and blue. The purse and shoes were beige or a tan brown. I knew the dress was an Alexander McQueen, because a chic on the beach I used to date had the same kind, but hers was a different color. She was a cutie, and she was an eye doctor. She kept saying her father paid a grip for the dress as a gift for her getting her degree. Her shades were gold trimmed, and she had a long black ponytail going down her back. I knew it was a weave, but the shit looked fly. Sexy redbone and either she had her own doe or some fool was spending on her.

She walked right up to Laylow's door, knocking loudly. Damn, is Laylow fucking this chic? Shorty was looking like a tall glass of orange juice, and a nigga was thirsty because she was ghetto sexy.

I got out my car to speak to her. "Um, I'm sorry, miss. Uh, Laylow just left. If you want, I can tell him you came through," I said, flicking my dreads over my shoulder. When she walked towards me, I swear I recognized her, but from where?

"Yes," she said, sashaying with a sexy walk like a runway model. "Please tell Anthony I want my cut for those rims I helped him get. You know I pointed him in the right direction. Like a finder's fee." Then she smiled and walked closer to me. Taking off her shades, staring at me with green eyes, she said, "Do I know you, handsome?" She looked me up and down. Then it hit me where I knew her from.

"Damn, Gina!" I said out loud, but more to myself than to her.

"Um, excuse me?" she said, confused.

"I mean, what's up, Shavonda? Can I have my license now or what?" I said in a cocky manner.

"Mmph, mmph, hmmm, Mr. Baxter. As a matter of fact, I can have it for you first thing in the morning," she said, looking around in my Caprice. "Where is Julia Roberts at?" she grinned.

"Who?" I asked.

"The white chic. Isn't that your girl?" she said, playing with her ponytail. Shorty was built like Lisa Raye but favored Tisha Campbell. Body banging. I mean, nice breasts, but she had a huge booty. You could sit a glass of water on it.

"Naw. She is a polite acquaintance, but she is not my girlfriend. Haven't had nothing like that in a while," I said, realizing she had walked up so close I could have kissed her.

"Baby, your problem is that you haven't had a grown-ass woman to help you with that. By the way, I'm going for a bite," she said, walking towards her cherry red BMW. She looked back and asked, "Care to join me?" She got in her car and pulled beside mine.

I got in my car and rolled my windows down. "Lead the way, beautiful. By the way, my friends call me Yayo or Yay for short," I said, cranking up the Caprice.

"Hmmm... Yay, huh? Well, I like your name, but I know how the streets go. So just follow me," she said, putting her shades back on.

"By the way, if you don't mind me asking, how do you know Laylow?" I said, nodding my head to Kevin Gates.

"Who, Anthony? Boy, that's my nephew. I used to be married to his uncle, but that was a long time ago." She took a deep breath, then looked at me with a slick smile on her face. Then she licked her lips. "Now I'm just having fun." She said, "Oh, I'm paying for our meal. I got my own, boo."

"Okay. After we eat, sexy, what's next?" I said, smiling my gold-toothed smile.

"That's simple, baby, dessert!" she said and pulled off, and I followed behind her, feeling like the don I am.

Chapter 11

Getting It In...

I can't lie. I was having a good time with Shavonda. She was born in New York, but she was a resident of Virginia Beach. Once we got to Virginia, I parked my car in a twenty-four-hour parking lot. On the strip you have to pay for parking. It's just the way it is. I put the tag on my rearview mirror. It showed I paid for the space. I got out and walked to a nice restaurant called Peabody's. I had passed it a thousand times and never went in.

We were seated and the waiter came over. Obviously, you had to have reservations just to eat there. Shavonda, however, was a regular.

My drink was Grey Goose on ice. She ordered a Charles Woodson. It's wine. I think it's a football player for the Raiders that endorsed it, but I'm not sure. She told me she had been divorced three years ago, but her ex-husband finally left her alone just a little over a year ago. On her left hand was a nasty burn. She had a tattoo covering it that said, *3rd Degree* with a number three, the word degree written in Old English letters.

I didn't ask, but she caught me looking. She took another sip of her drink and said, "A parting gift from my ex-husband. Some men can't take the word no." She then said she had worked for the DMV because he had gotten her a job there. Melvin Skinner was his name, and he was older than her. No kids, "Thank God," she said.

Shavonda was doing a little modeling here and there. But after the burn on her hand it wasn't the same. She had a lawsuit she won from the DMV in Richmond where the incident happened. She had constantly told her supervisor about Melvin bothering and harassing her at work. They ignored her though, and Melvin spilled hot coffee on her hand on purpose. Another coworker had witnessed it and testified on her behalf. So, she left New York two years ago and she moved to Virginia. She got a job with the D.M.V in Elizabeth City. As far as the money, she bought herself a little cottage on the beach as well as the Beamer. That was a year ago.

Even though Melvin did a little jail time, he still had family in the Moyock and Edenton area. But they still treated her like family. So, Laylow would hook her up with plasma screen TVs and furniture. The rims came from a guy who wanted her, but she only flirted with him to get them cheaper for Laylow. He owed her three hundred dollars. The rims were fly though, but Laylow had promised if she talked the dude down, he had her.

"Fool will probably try to give me some more stolen shit." We both laughed.

"So, if that girlfriend is not your girlfriend, then what's the deal? You seem pretty laid back, but you a heartbreaker," she said, asking the waiter to fill my glass.

"It's complicated, I guess. We just exist and it works for us. I thought of fucking with her like that, but she still too loose. So, it is what it is," I said, thanking the waiter and then sipping my Avion tequila.

"You are so sweet. I know exactly why it's like that though," she said knowingly while eating her salad. I had fried salmon with lemon juice smothered on it, with a nice helping of shrimp on the side.

"Okay, Ms. Cleo, then tell me why I chill with her?" I replied.

"Okay," she said, wiping her mouth with her napkin. "I saw her, and she is sexy. But in a trashy way. You, boo, got it going on and somehow your paths crossed. She is a lost soul, and you help her in your own way. But you know if you fall in love with her, she will disappoint you." She sipped her wine and held up a well-manicured finger. "Also, she doesn't want to lose you because obviously, you know her flaws. But she cannot keep you because of her flaws. Therefore, it's like a constant stalemate."

I was quiet for a while because Shavonda had pulled my whole card. Shit, that's exactly how I felt. So, it was confusing me why Milk Marie was being so emotional lately.

Shavonda looked at me sadly and said, "I'm sorry, Yay. I didn't mean to hit a nerve, boo. But if she could have kicked my ass, she would have. I usually don't flirt that openly, but," she bit her lip, "damn boy, you are a cutie. So that chic must got issues. I'm just saying."

"Naw, ma, you good. You females are amazing to me. You got all that out of seeing me at the DMV, huh?" I smirked, the liquor on me.

"Yes and everything happens for a reason. I didn't even have to wait for your cute ass to come get your license. I mean what's the odds?" she said blowing a kiss at me from across the table.

Once we left the restaurant, we walked down the boardwalk. We talked about everything from music, food, and type of weed. I had a blunt already rolled, but you had to be careful smoking on the beach in Virginia. We walked the beach, puffing and laughing, when we saw other people turn their noses up to the smell. Surprisingly, we weren't far from her cottage.

It was nice not to think of the streets, Han Che, and other issues for a while. Plus, I was bugging off guys turning their heads because Shavonda's ass was out this world. I would palm her ass ever now and then as we walked. So, niggas could hate. In a cute voice she would say, "You are so nasty, Yay." Then she would whisper in my ear, "I like that about you."

I thought, *it's about to go down. I'm about to get it, and smash shorty for real.* Some girls walked by looking at me, whispering, then giggling. I felt Shavonda grab the bulge in my pants and say, "Sorry, ladies. He is mine tonight."

The girls giggled. One said, "You go, girl." Another yelled, "Lucky bitch."

Once we got to her house and were inside, I could not front. Her shit was dope. The living room was huge. There was an all-white couch in the shape of half a damn circle that took up the whole damn living room. There were pictures of Malcolm X, Marvin Gaye, Miles Davis, Billie Holiday, Marcus Garvey, and Martin Luther King all over the walls of the spacious living room. It had gotten a little chilly outside, and the warmth of the fireplace was helping the liquor come alive in my veins.

I wanted her. That big ass was in the air as she replaced the screen in front of the fire. Shavonda knew I was watching her. She walked me into the hallway to show me around some more. There were pictures of Prince on the walls. There was one of Rick James and Tina Marie. The bathroom was black and red, with a Chinese shower curtain, bathmat, and pictures of dragons covered the walls.

We finally got to her bedroom. A brass sitting chair and table with all kinds of perfumes by J-Lo, Chanel, Liz Claiborne, Beyoncé, etc., were on display. She had a walk-in closet. When you turned the light on, there was a button that made all of her outfits rotate until she pressed another button to make them stop. Shoes, high heels, all in glass cases that were stacked to the ceiling. This chic had a big ass chandelier hanging over the bed, small crystal hearts made up the chandelier. Yo, her spot was fly! She even had a mini bar next to her bathroom that was also in the big bedroom.

"What you think of the word cottage?"

I thought it meant a small version of a house. "This shit is fly, Shavonda!" I still was looking around.

She blushed and was pleased by my response to her home. She said she created everything based off of what she liked. She brought us two glasses of orange juice spiked with Grey Goose. I didn't drink brown, and neither did she. I liked that.

"I've never brought anyone here. I mean, I've had a few flings, but not one seemed to penetrate my mind to allow them here," she said, sipping her drink and then putting it beside her on the nightstand.

"So, how did I get lucky? Because, honestly, I'm the same. No one knows where I live." Then the thought of Han Che dropping me off at the apartment filled my mind. "Well, almost no one," I said, downing my drink. She took the glass from me, and she put it on the nightstand with hers. God, she was gorgeous. Though I was sure she was older than me, I had no plans of asking her and finding out. I always learned less brings more.

As if she read my thoughts, her dress dropped to the floor. Her ass was so phat that I could see it from the front. I think I remember Mos Def saying that in a song and now I knew what he meant. She had on a maroon Victoria's Secret bra and panties set that matched. She kept her heels on. She looked at me and said, "You've flirted with me all night, even felt me up. But you haven't kissed me. That's so rude," she said, stepping closer to me. I kicked my Jordans off, then dropped my pants. She looked at the bulge in my boxers. "Oh, yes, mommy is going to take real good care of you." I stepped closer to her.

"I apologize for my rudeness. Let me make it up to you."
I started kissing her, our tongues everywhere.

"Yes! Yay, man... baby, you want this pussy, boy?" she
said playfully, pushing me back. She turned around, smacked
her ass, and crawled onto the bed like a panther. She put her
face down with her big ass up high in the air and said, "Now
come and get your dessert." She shook her ass, taunting me.
I put my whole face in her ass, eating her from the back.
"Mmm, Yay, shit yeah, stick your tongue in it. Oh shit, you
so nasty," she said, bumping her ass against my face. I had
my left hand on her left cheek, right hand on her right cheek,
and face buried in the crack of her ass. "I'm cumming, shit,
I'm cumming on your tongue."

I couldn't stand it. I was harder than a brick. Before I
could put it in her, she laid on her back rubbing her clit. She
said, "Get up here and feed momma that dick." I walked
over her, sat on her chest, and fucked her mouth. She was
devouring me. "Mmm yes, mmmm, this my dick tonight,"
she said between sucking me. Shorty was a freak. I flipped
her over, and then I slapped her ass. "Oh shit, nigga. Represent on this pussy" she said as I put every inch of me inside
her. She felt so good. I pounded her for what felt like hours.
The way DMX fucked Kesha in *Belly* times three for real.

"Oh shit, mmm, it's too damn much, boo," she said biting hard into a pillow.

"Shut up and take this dick! You like that, huh?" I was
in a frenzy. I thought of my life, about being an orphan, and
my parents dead. I came from nothing. Life had always
fought me, but I always fought back. I took it all out on
Shavonda's pussy.

"Shit, oh, I'm cumming. I'm about to bust," I said, sweat
pouring down my face.

"Cum for me, don't fucking take it out this pussy."

"Say my damn name then," I grunted, busting all in her.

"Yay, man, Yayo, shit!" We both were drenched in sweat.

I had my hand resting on her ass like it was a damn coffee table. I rolled over, and we both were just staring at one another.

"Boo, I don't know what you've been going through, but please feel free to take it on this pussy. Lord have mercy," she said giggling.

"Yo, ma, you got booty for days. I felt like I was riding a bull," I said, catching my breath, rolling a blunt I got out my pants pocket on the floor.

We smoked.

"What happened to your shoulder? I used to be a nurse. Take that shirt off and let me fix you up," she said, getting a First Aid kit. She cleaned my wound, rewrapped it in clean bandages, and it actually felt better.

"I know we don't really know each other, but Yayo, you seem to be a really smart guy. This thug shit is a turn on, but I hope whatever this is, you can resolve it. And we can get closer. From what you told me, you got part ownership in a thirty-apartment duplex. Boy, you don't need to be shooting or getting shot," she said as we laid in her big bed. "You need to be in Armani in an office on some boss shit." She was smoking the blunt, making O's with the smoke.

"I feel that, but once I figure out who killed my boy and get my funds straight, I'm out of here," I said, thinking I should leave once things got straightening out. But I loved Virginia. In this game, if you can get out and have no fed time and have money put up, go. But the life, like the same drugs we sold, was an addiction.

"Well, for now," she said, putting the blunt out, "I'm down for round two."

"Shit, don't talk about it," I said, slapping her ass, and she rode me until we fell asleep.

Chapter 12

Everything Happens for A Reason...

I awoke feeling well rested and well fucked. I smelled eggs and pancakes. I got up, walked down the hallway, and into the living room. It was to my left. The kitchen was to my right. She had bar stools, about five, around a marble countertop. She had no stove, but a flat top to cook on and an oven in the wall.

"What's up, sleepy head? I know a lot of brothas don't eat the swine. You seem to be a non-pork brotha," she said, wearing a Balenciaga robe on with printed hundred-dollar bills all over it. There was a long, glass table to the left of the marble counter, with eight seats around it. It looked as if it were just for show.

"You keep being all sexy with breakfast, it might be hard to leave," I said as I took the plate of egg whites, toast with jelly, grits, and beef sausage. She was pouring me a glass of orange juice.

"I don't remember telling you that you had to leave. But all I ask is don't be a stranger. Not after what you did to me last night." She smirked with a big titty falling out of her robe. A nigga had to be careful. I thought on what Han Che had said.

"Do you like apples, Shavonda?" I said for no reason.

"Hell no! I only like shit like oranges, cantaloupe, and of course bananas," she said, glancing at my crotch.

I had on only boxers. I never got comfortable like that with anyone. Most chics, I would already be dressed and gone. But something about Shavonda was genuine and real. So I went with my gut, as I always did. "Girl, you nasty," I said, eating my eggs.

"And you made me that way." She smirked.

"You were already a freak. It just took me to get you to just be you," I said.

"Takes one to know one, boo," she said, walking around the counter, booty everywhere, and loving my eyes on her. "I like the way you look at me. I'm serious, though, I want to get to know you." She sipped my orange juice.

"That's cool, but I got to handle some things I hope will give us the chance," I said playfully, taking my orange juice back after devouring my plate. She pouted playfully.

"Baby, um, you know you talk in your sleep a little bit? You kept saying something about Russians and Han or something." She got up and took my plate. She started to tidy up the kitchen. "That was your friend, right? This Han guy," she said, wiping the counter.

"Yeah, that's him," I said, rubbing my right shoulder, which was starting to feel better.

Shavonda handed me my painkillers and said to me, "I washed your clothes, and they are out the dryer laid out in the living room. Got your pills and this. She dug into the pocket of her robe and tossed me a wad of money in a spider web of rubber bands. "Nigga, why you got enough to put in a bank account in your pocket?" she said, shaking her head.

"Well, because if I get locked up, or ever on the highway and my car breaks down, I want to be prepared for anything. That way I got emergency money on me," I said, putting the money back on the counter.

"Bet you don't even know how much it is," Shavonda said.

I replied, "Three thousand, four hundred and sixty-seven dollars and I think sixty cents," I said, smiling.

She put six dimes on the counter, laughing. "As I said, you're too smart for the life you're in. I hope you solve the issue. It's weird though," she said, biting her purple polished nails.

"What's weird, sexy?" I said, getting up and stretching, and then walking into the living room to get my clothes.

"Well, I do have my own hustle, other than middleman on items from the person or persons I link up with. For a nice price, I can get you a fake ID. A few days before I met you, my girl tells me the person. They don't know me, and I never meet them. I get the picture, and I come up with a new name. My girl is out there a little, but she said it was for Nikoli, her new playmate." Then she whispered into the phone that this Nikoli dude had deep pockets, but a little dick.

I had finished getting dressed in the living room and started putting myself down. "Boo, that big ass gun is in the drawer beside the bed." She walked up to me and said, "Baby, did you hear what I said?"

"Yeah, your girl got some little dick dude named Nikoli tricking on her." My mind was elsewhere. I felt I was slipping because I felt laid back with Shavonda. She wasn't one of those hood rat type chics to check your pockets or do grimy shit.

Aunt Nancy used to tell me, "Sooner or later, you have to trust someone, nephew." Then I caught on to what Shavonda was saying.

"Vonda, are you saying this clown you made the ID for is Russian?" I said, all ears now walking toward the bedroom. Even my holster was in the drawer. I strapped up.

She said, while getting dressed, "Honey, I don't know any black dudes with a name like Nikoli, do you?" She slipped on a Burberry top with pants that matched. No heels. She had some Burberry slip-ons that looked like Vans. Damn, shorty could clean up.

"Baby, tell me you keep some kind of file on the IDs you make," I said, a little excited.

"Sweetheart, I'm way ahead of you." Shavonda walked over to the walk-in closet and opened a small file cabinet. She walked over and handed a picture to me. It was a baldheaded white-looking guy with a scruffy looking beard. He looked like he had a tattoo of a sword piercing an eye with little drops of dripping blood. I stared at the picture and said, "Are you the motherfucka that killed Han?"

"What you say, baby?" Shavonda said, shutting her closet.

"Nothing, boo. Look I got to go," I said, kissing her and hating I had to leave.

"Yay, I'm off today. I'm just going in to get your ID. Matter of fact, give me your phone." She took it out my hands and programmed her number into it under Vonda with a heart emoji. I palmed that ass with both hands and kissed her again. I walked to the door.

"Oh, Yay, hold up," she said, biting her lips.

"What's up, ma?" I said, folding the paper up in my pocket.

"My girl said the dude, Nikoli, has a really bad limp. He told her a dog bit him or some shit. Just remembered it. I don't know if that helps." She said looking for her keys. It was like 11:00 am, and I had a few missed calls. I'd check them once I left.

"Has a really bad limp, huh? Dog bit him, but did she say where?" I said, wondering if it was the clown I shot in the ass. If it was, then it was the same bastard that killed Han.

"I don't know where, but I think his hip or some shit. My girl is really a thotty kind of chic," she said, finding her keys.

"Damn, boo, you might have solved a lot of my issues. For real, ma," I said, opening the door.

"Hey, Yay!" she yelled as I was walking out the door.

"What's up, Vonda?" I said, tryin to bounce.

"Everything happens for a reason, sexy. You better call me, okay?" she said, blowing a kiss to me.

"I got you, ma, trust that." I winked at her and shut the door. I ran to my car, and as I was doing a light jog, I thought, we *might at least know what the fools look like*. It was all about getting the other two and getting Han Che's coke back.

I made it to my Caprice and ripped the twenty-four-hour parking paper off the rearview mirror. I took the picture out and stuck it on the dashboard. On my way back to Moyock, I stared at the picture to burn the guy's face into my brain.

"It's on, Han," I said out loud in the car.

Everything happens for a reason indeed!

Fre$h

Chapter 13

Revenge Is Mine...

I had missed calls from Milk Marie, Patron, and a number I didn't know. I called the number I did not recognize first but blocked my number. Jay-Z's music played about coughing up a lung in Marcy Projects. Then a familiar voice answered.

"Yo, who is this, and why are you calling me blocked? Sharlene, is this you playing on my phone?"

"Nigga, it's Yay, fool, and I didn't know your number because I didn't have it saved in my phone. So, what's good?" I said, starting my Caprice.

"What's good is it's on, nigga. Amanda 'Good Pussy' Sanders said them fools is holed up in the beach house. Now she made it clear they got heat. I think a bunch of Uzis and a few handguns," Laylow said.

"Damn, these niggas real brave. Only three of them, and I know they still got my goods. Okay, like Phil Collins said, 'Tonight's The Night.' I'll get up with Polo in a few. Good lookin, my gee," I said, pulling up at Sonic just to park. Some teenager with braces on, wearing roller skates was coming toward my car. I waved her off.

"Naw, Yay. Come on, dawg. I'm the one that sniffed these niggas out. I know how you get down, but it's three of them niggas and three of us. My heart don't pump no Kool-Aid, bruh. I'm tryin to eat," Laylow said, desperate to get in on the lick.

I'd rather have Patron on deck, but this was some right-now shit. It was a little past noon, and Laylow was cool, but Patron I trusted. But he said something next that convinced me.

"Look, Yay, Amanda 'Good Pussy' Sanders loves me, dawg. I been waxing that ass for a minute. She said she going over there around 11:00 pm. One of these dudes always crashes in the living room. Upstairs is two bedrooms. One of them is spending paper on her. The bitch gave me a thousand dollars after I hit that Mandingo style." Laylow laughed.

"Okay, bet then, homie. What we going to do if we creep them fools. Tell Amanda to let us know an hour after she has been there, where everyone is in position at in the house. Tell her to text only you and delete every text message. Once they are in a position where we think we can take them, text her a bunch of dots like a period after a sentence. That means we going in. I need to know what kind of gun you got and Polo," I said, pushing the red button on the Sonic sign and ordering a large tea.

"Why you want to know what kind of guns we got?" Laylow said, obviously not experienced.

"You'll see when we link up tonight. Now hit Polo and let him know what's up. I'll hit you back tonight," I said, letting the chic with braces keep the change.

"I got you, Yay. Say no more. One," he said.

"One," I said and hung up.

I called Patron, but he didn't pick up. I texted Polo and told him to link up with Laylow. Then my phone rang with Future singing, "Chase a check, never chase a bitch."

"Yo, what's up, my gee?" I said to Patron.

"I'm in Richmond, my nigga. Got a good deal on a few pounds of Triple O-Gee. What's good your way?" Patron replied.

"Coolin, coolin. Remember that chic I told you I met at the DMV?" I asked.

"Yeah, the chic you say thick like Lisa Raye, but look like Gina off *Martin*?" he said laughing.

"Yeah. Yo, shorty a damn freak, my nigga. Booty for days and shorty got a fly crib. Yo homie, broad cooked me breakfast," I said, sipping my tea.

"Breakfast? Breakfast, say it ain't so, O.G. Ah man, when the last time you spend the night with a chic? Shorty must be got that fire," Patron said, laughing.

"Man, I haven't spent the night since Tracy got me for three hundred out my pants. That was two years ago, when we were still selling ounces. I'm, telling you, shorty on fleek, my dude," I said, leaning back in the Caprice.

"Cool, cool. But what about Milk Marie, Yay? That snow bunny love you, man. Shit, she hit me up this morning looking for that ass. I know you two not exactly boo'd up, but chics still be in they feelings when they still getting the dick, playa," Patron replied.

"Man kill that noise, Pe. She be fuckin niggas and don't forget she went MIA on a nigga for a week. Besides, I got that Section 8 spot we use to cook up in. I'm thinking about letting her stay there. Can't make no hoe into a housewife homie." I said rolling some purple up.

"Preeeaaaccchhhh!" Patron said, quoting a Young Dolph song, "Damn, you still got that spot in Herrington Village? You be holding out, my dude."

"Naw. Never that, pimp. We just been doing so good this year. It's been two months since I used it. Why cook it up when we got thirty a bird, and we paying fifteen a bird? Shit, I haven't sold crack in so long, I damn near feel like Jay," I said, confident.

"You still got that boy in the grave?" Patron said in code.

"Yeah, I buried that body months ago for a rainy day. Shit, you better do the same," I said. The "body" was one million I had buried in Aunt Nancy's backyard. She didn't even know it was there. *Always think ahead*, Han would say. Thinking of Han made me realize why I hit up Patron.

"Yo, I think I got a line on those fools that smoked Han and leaned my damn right shoulder," I said.

"Damn and you just calling me now?" I heard Patron cocking his nine. "I liked Han's *Karate Kid* looking ass. What's the plan, O.G.?"

"The plan is for you to handle your B.I. Don't rush back here with all that grass, homie. I got two shooters. I'm good," I said.

"Fuck them. I'm a sniper, and I still got your present gift wrapped. But you keep me posted. For real, Yay. You my big brother. I love yo ass, no homo. Broke niggas make noise," Patron said.

"Rich niggas make money," I replied and hung up.

I put my head back on the seat. I didn't want to call Milk Marie. What was up with her calling Patron anyway? Truth was, I was tired and going to go home and get my mind right. I pulled out and called my man, Pedro. He was my car man who had painted my BMW. I needed to lay shit out and be precise like chess.

"Pedro's paint shop. You pay it. We spray it," he said in English, but Spanish ruled with his words.

"Pedro, it's Yay, homie."

"Hey, my friend. What can I do for you? Is this your new line to reach you?" Pedro said.

"Yeah, look on 115 Harris Drive. There will be a rusty, burgundy Caprice sitting in a parking space with a 'Y' in yellow in the parking spot. Keys will be in the glove compartment. Paint it midnight black and make the tint a bit darker," I said, pulling up to the apartment.

"You mean the apartment duplex out in Prie Town?" Pedro said.

"Yeah. That's the place. How long before it's all done?" I said, looking at my G-Shock.

"Uh, let's see. It's going on one. So how about six pm? I'll have it back in the same parking spot, Vato," he said.

"Si, Papi." It sounded like a plan. "Just hit my line when it's back in the same parking spot. Oh, how much I owe you?" I said to Pedro.

"I heard about your hospital visit. You know the price for the tint, but the paint job is on me. Just stop getting shot, Yay. You my best customer," Pedro said.

"Thanks, Papi. I hit you with the dinero manana, okay?" I said.

"Si, Yayo. You take care. Hasta pronto." Then he hung up.

I put the keys in the glove compartment and went to the elevator. I took the picture off the dashboard of this Nikoli character. Why the fuck were Russians robbing us? Also, how did they know about the meet? I saw the interest in Han Che's eyes when I told him anybody come around speaking Russian, I was popping them.

I made a note to try to learn different languages in the future. Shit, I'm sure it would come in handy. I knew enough Spanish because of school, and Pedro would help me out. But damn, Chinese and now Russian. Goes to show drugs come from outside the country. Didn't matter those fools are going to feel these hot ones tonight. Bet that!

I got to my floor, which was the fourth. It was a six-floor duplex with five apartments on each floor. It had been built in 1968, and I liked the old-school look. It reminded me of the apartments from the sitcom, *The Jeffersons*. I never really went to the balcony, went out to smoke and put half the blunt out. I could tell Milk Marie had been there. A note was on the fridge. It said, "Thanks for letting me know you're okay." I balled it up because I wasn't in the mood for sarcasm. I looked at the view I had, and I remembered there was a time when I'd loved it. The waterfront stretched out among the city.

I think it stretched from the Atlantic. I wasn't sure. I loved being surrounded by al that water. Now, I was thinking of relocating. But where? Then I thought of Shavonda and smiled. Most females around here were from all different colleges, looking for fun and a sugar daddy. Even though I was only twenty-three years old, I wanted a chic who was smart, successful, and a freak in the sheets but a woman in public. The thing with Milk Marie was fun, but I was mad at myself. I loved her, but I could not be in love with her.

Though I understood her, she wasn't trying to get her life together. I felt like after months of fun, she was changing for me. It's like trying to be like Ice-T in *New Jack City*. Remember when he took Pookie to rehab? Yeah, Pookie was clean for a while, but he didn't allow the love Ice-T showed him to help him overcome his addiction. Pookie got some dope on the sly, got high, and it cost him. I was Ice-T, and Milk Marie was my Pookie.

See, meeting me put her in rehab. A place to stay, the Tahoe, and it looked like a real relationship. But once I started asking her to get her GED, to try to get custody of her kids and to step up, I was messing up the moment. I had businesses, money stashed, and so I always thought ahead. I don't even think Milk Marie had a bank account. I remember the first three months. She gave her mom my number. Why I don't know, when she had a phone.

"This is Yay. Who am I speaking with?" Me and Patron were in the cook-up apartment then.

"This is Tina. Tina Murphy. Is Shayla around you, Yay?" she said with an attitude.

"Um, no ma'am. I can give her a message. You don't have her number, Mrs. Murphy?" I said, bagging up ounces.

"Her number, huh? I didn't even know she had a phone. Well, you tell her I said this the third weekend she promised to get these kids, and she hasn't showed." Mrs. Murphy was pissed.

I could hear the boys in the background. "Is that Mom, Grandma? Is she coming, Granny?"

I was pissed because she had eight hundred dollars, and I never asked her where she got the money. But she was trying to get a car. Pedro had an old Tahoe, all-black, that he was trying to get rid of. But he wanted fifteen hundred for the truck. I bought the truck. Pedro had repainted it. The interior was a bit rough, because it was actually his wife's truck. They had seven kids, all different ages of course. So, the truck had history. I told Milk Marie to give me the eight hundred. Then I walked her outside to see her new truck.

"Damn, Yay! You didn't have to do that. I know it cost more than eight hundred. So, what do I owe you?" she said, looking at the paint job.

"It's a bit of wear and tear in the inside, but it's straight. Plus, you don't owe me nothing. It's to have enough room for your kids," I said.

Her mood changed. "Yeah, my mom been getting on me. I should have never used your BMW to go see them. She swears I got money now. I told her about you, but she is a mess. She would practically pull up, leave the kids here, and drive off," she said, in the truck now and messing with the radio.

"No offense, but please never tell her where I live. But now you got room to scoop your kids," I said to her, knowing we weren't actually a couple.

What we had worked at that time. I got that truck a month before her mom called me. I told her about the phone call. She gave me some excuse, but I blew it off. I still believed I was helping her like Han and Aunt Nancy had helped me.

Months later, we were tight, and I brought up seeing her kids. She got mouthy about trying to be in her business, but that her mom was complicated. Excuses were like assholes. Everyone has one. Shit was a turn off, like J Cole said, 'Don't save her, she don't want to be saved.' That's why I was different, and Shavonda made me look at a lot of chics. Sex is sex, but when someone motivates you to be better, that is a relationship.

I left the balcony, closed and locked the sliding door, put the half of a blunt in the ashtray, and kicked my Jordans off. I took off my Levi's and eased out of my t-shirt. I set my Philadelphia Eagles alarm clock that my aunt and bought me for my birthday last year. You could even load up to ten songs in it as alarm ringtones. I looked at the medallion with my mom's picture in it, and she was beautiful.

I let the chain drop down my chest and pulled my green covers back, exhausted. I popped two painkillers and fell into a coma.

My dream was weird because it was dark, and I could hear someone calling my name. It was a female's voice. She called to me, using my real name.

"Seemiyun, I love you, son. Please listen to me. You have to be careful. They know more than you know."

"Mu, muh, Mom… Is that you?" Then I could see her, but a vague image of her, she looked like Claire Huxtable off

The Cosby Show. "I miss you! I know you didn't give me up for adoption. Aunt Nancy told me everything. I wish I had known you," I said.

"Son, it's okay. I am always with you. I need you to listen to me. Your enemy is also your friend. Please be careful."

Then the vision of her was gone, and I was outside standing in the rain. There was no one in the BMW. I knew where I was now. The spot we got jacked at in Moyock. I heard feet running the other way. The rain was pounding my face, and I could barely see. I was holding Han in my arms. I could feel my right shoulder burning. We were both up against this black Benz. Han's eyes were closed, and I kept calling his name.

I looked up from Han, and I saw Milk Marie in the distance. She was trying to tell me something. She was pointing and it looked like she was yelling. But no words were coming out of her mouth. The rain was pouring, and I kept yelling, "What? I can't hear you, Marie." Then I looked back at Han and his eyes were open.

I jumped out my sleep, and I felt sweat beading on my forehead. *What the fuck?* I thought. But before I woke up and Han's eyes were open, I heard him say, "Revenge is mine!"

Fre$h

Chapter 14

Ride or Die...

I was in the shower trying to make sense of the dream. Can't lie, the dream had me really fucked up. Plus, my mom was warning me that my enemy was my friend. Well, good thing I didn't have many friends. Damn could it be Patron, Milk Marie, or Polo? Shit, maybe even Han Che himself?

I had to keep my mind clear. It was close to time to ride on these fools. Dream or no dream, I was going to handle mine. I got out the shower, pulled the plastic bag from around my right shoulder, put my Hilfiger boxers and all-gray Hilfiger socks on, and then I put on an all-black, long-sleeved shirt. I got some all-black Dickies and a button-up shirt. My black Timbs finished my attire.

I went to the closet and pushed the button on the wall. I had a duffel bag on the bed. I kept my Desert Eagle on me. When the false wall moved, it exposed my arsenal.

I took a Glock 45, night goggles, extra ammo and of course, my vest. I zipped up the duffel bag and my alarm started playing Future, "Turn out the lights/I'm looking for/I'm looking for." I turned off the alarm. It was ten pm. We had an hour and a half ride to Corolla on the beach. Before closing the wall, I grabbed three silencers from the closet. I pressed the button and pushed my clothes on the hangers back in place to cover the small black button.

There was a closet in the hallway. I allowed, over time, Milk Marie to put some of her clothes in it. My excuse was I had a closet full. Since we didn't know how things were between us, she didn't mind.

I checked my phone. Laylow had a 9mm. Polo had a 45, and I had my Desert Eagle, as well as my 45. I checked the inscriptions on the silencers, nodded to myself, and then put them in the duffel bag. I sent a text message to Laylow and Polo telling them to be ready. I was picking them up from Laylow's spot.

I heard the door close. I grabbed the duffel bag, and I walked into the living room. Milk Marie was standing there. I gently put the duffel bag on the couch.

"Well, hello stranger. I thought you almost didn't live here anymore." Then she looked at my clothing, the duffel bag, and back at me. "Yay, before you go out there all Rambo, we need to talk," she said with her hands on her hips.

"Hold on." I ran into the bedroom to retrieve a special item. I came back in the living room, looking at my G-shock. "Look, Milk Marie, whatever there is, it's got to wait. I got so much on my plate, it's not even funny. Okay?"

"Why didn't you come home the other night?" she said, sitting on the arm of the couch.

"Are you fucking serious right now? Marie, last time I checked, we not married. One night isn't a week either. We fuck. We chill. We play house. But you got shit to deal with in your life, and I got mine."

"I'm sorry. Okay. Shit with my kids, my life, my mom… it's complicated. You wouldn't understand. You got all this." She waved around the apartment, "I've fucked guys just to have a place to stay before I met you."

"Fuck you, Milk. I was an orphan. My best friend got adopted with me, and I met an aunt who could barely take care of both of us. So, all of this," I waved, mimicking her action, "came from me getting off my ass and handling mine. Nobody gave me shit. I have tried to help you, and you threw a tantrum and went out. I'm good. No hard feelings, okay? Damn," I said, grabbing the duffel bag and heading for the door. My right shoulder was throbbing. I was too damn mad to show it. I didn't have time for this soap opera, Spanish novella bullshit right now.

"Damn it, Yayo! I fucking love you," Milk Marie said with tears spilling from her eyes. I turned to look at her. "Please stay here and let's talk. I don't want to just play house anymore. I have something important to tell you."

I was thrown off guard because I've only seen her cry one time and now this one. My heart was thawing out a little. But then I thought of the week she had been gone, I kept silently hoping she would be in the apartment. I never called her, but she never called me either. I even called her mom, but I never told her that. "Yay, you seen like a nice guy, but my daughter isn't one to sit still, if you know what I mean. At least, she's seen the kids more since she has known you," her mom told me when I called.

I turned and faced Milk with so much anger. I needed to save that anger for my foes. I said, "You know, if you had said that a few weeks ago, things would be different. But you got your life, and I got mine. You can have the apartment in Herrington Village. I tried, Shayla," I said, slamming the door.

I could hear her screams from the elevator all the way until I got outside. People were coming out of their apartments.

"Yay, please. Yay, don't go. Yay!"

It hurt me to leave on those terms but is what it is. Don't know what the hell got into Milk Marie. I put the duffel bag on the hood of a car, looking for mine, not realizing this was my car. The Caprice was blacker than Wesley Snipes. I even had black rims. I could see my reflection in the fifteen percent tint.

"Damn, Pedro. You the man!" I said to myself. Got the keys out the glove box, popped the trunk, and put the duffel bags in. I got the hell out of there before the neighbors thought it was some domestic violence shit going on.

As I was cruising to Laylow's spot, a note was on my dash. It said, "You know the price for the tint. I had the rims lying around the shop. Thought you'd like them. I know what all-black means. Be careful, primo. La familia, Pedro." I ripped the note up and threw it out the window. I sent a text to Patron and told him to give Pedro two grams first thing tomorrow when he got back from Richmond. I had a feeling it was going to be a long night. It was a Friday night, so the beach would be buzzing. Hopefully, it would camouflage our actions.

I picked up Laylow and Polo, then kept pushing it to the beach.

"Yo, when you get the Caprice? This shit dope, Yay. Thought you were the damn D.T., shit so black." Polo laughed.

"That's what took you fools so long to come outside?" I said, shaking my head.

"Man, I boost my ass off, Yay. I didn't know who it was. If you wouldn't have texted it was you outside, I probably would have crept out the back," Laylow said, making us laugh. "Oh! By the way, playboy, my aunt told me to give you this," Laylow said, handing me a small, yellow envelope.

I opened it and it had my license in it. There was a piece of paper attached that read, "Here is your credentials. Don't be a stranger. My bed misses you – Vonda." It even had a lipstick print on it. I smiled and threw the note and the envelope out the window.

Smiling to myself, I slipped my ID in the ashtray of the car and closed it. I never smoked in any of my cars, nor did I smoke cigarettes. It was such a nasty habit. I turned my head and these fools were both staring at me grinning, "What the hell you smiling at?" I asked with a little attitude.

"Yo, Yay, you a smooth nigga. I fuck with you the long way. But nigga, I'm not calling you Uncle Yayo." I tried not to laugh, but we all busted out laughing.

"Now homie, if it's an issue," I said matter of factly.

"Yo, playboy, kill that. My uncle fucked that up a long time ago. But be careful, dawg. Shavonda a cougar," Laylow said.

"Shit, that white girl going to kill you, bruh. Milk Marie a little trashy, but she like a thotty Selena Gomez," Polo said rolling a blunt.

"First of all, you not lighting that shit in my ride. Second of all, Milk Marie isn't my girl. We just exist in the same space."

Polo and Laylow looked at each other and said, at the same time, "Fuck buddies," and then started laughing.

I shook my head at these two knuckleheads. "Can you two please get focused? We will be there soon. These fools tried to take out all three of us that night. I'm thirsty right now, homie, and it's not for no chic," I said with murder in my eyes.

The car was quiet for a minute. Then all I heard was Laylow's nine and Polo's 45 cocking back. I nodded my head to them both. "Now you speaking my language, homies." I said, turning up the French Montana and Rick Ross song, "Stay Schemin" on the radio. "Stay schemin/niggas trying to get at me/Dawg I ride for my niggas."

Fre$h

Chapter 15

In the Cut...

We were parked three beach houses down from where the Russians were supposed to be holed up at. By now it was 11:45 at night, and the set-up seemed good. Amanda "Good Pussy" Sanders had a roommate named Tiffany. She was from Atlanta, and her mother had recently passed. Tiffany would be gone for at least two weeks. Laylow did damn good. He had the keys to the beach house. We all went in, only turning the living room lamp on.

Once I unzipped my duffel bag, I pulled out the night vision goggles. Then I gave both Polo and Laylow silencers, and I put several pair of latex gloves in my pocket. I passed both of them gloves and goggles. Then I gave them receiver buttons so we could speak without being loud. They looked like big, black buttons. Changed mine on my collar. Laylow put his in his hoodie. Polo put the receiver button on his sleeve. Then we all masked up.

I gently took out the grenade I went back for when Milk Marie started flipping her shit at me. Both Laylow and Polo had a fit for real when they saw it.

"My nigga, we been riding around with a fucking grenade in the car? Yayo, what the fuck, bruh? And where did you get all this secret ops military shit?" Polo said, putting the silencer on his 45.

"When this is over, you got to tell us. You evidently Batman for real," Laylow said. "This shit CIA be having."

"Let's just say I was really cool a while back with an arms dealer," I said, adjusting the goggles on my head. Then I pulled the box receiver out to test the buttons, which gave us a range at a thousand-mile radius. "Testing one, two, three," I said into my collar.

"Yo, this shit is dope. Yo, Yay, can I keep this shit?" Laylow said as he pressed the button to speak. "I'm on one, over," he said laughing.

"No and neither of you breathe a word you ever saw or had knowledge I have any this shit. Fuck the dope game. Getting caught with the silencers alone is fed time, fool. Not only that, we got night vision goggles and mini receivers," I said seriously.

"You right. You can get this back after we…" Laylow grabbed his phone and stopped talking. He then looked up, smiled at me, and said, "You ready for 1-8-7, my nigga?"

"Been ready, what's the verdict?" I said, suited up to the "T."

"Amanda said one is in the living room pacing and shit. The other one is upstairs sleeping. The guy she messing with is snorting coke in the bathroom," Laylow said.

I went outside and got my binoculars. I was watching a figure pace back and forth. He came outside to smoke. This was it, but we had to move.

"Let's go. Hit her with the dots. Laylow, take the fool that's outside smoking. Polo take care of the dude Amanda has in the bathroom. I'm climbing the balcony to creep in on sleeping beauty."

We took off running. Both beach houses in the middle were vacant. It was dark as hell. Someone was throwing a party a few blocks down. My adrenaline was pumping. I left the going up the side of the balcony where steps led up. I heard a loud gust of air right as I got to the top.

"One down, Yay. I'm on the bottom floor. Polo is going up to the bathroom," I heard Laylow say from my collar.

"Cool. Toss the living room. Look for the dope," I said.

"Roger that, homie," Laylow said.

"I'm at the bathroom," Polo said as I picked the lock on the sliding door. I saw a sleeping figure fully clothed, with a vodka bottle beside the bed. I was almost on him when I heard the sound of a door being kicked in. A female screamed, and then there was the unmistakable sound of gunfire.

Fuck… So much for the quiet approach. The guy woke up with a start as I put two in his chest. The Desert Eagle whistled. *PFF, PFF!*

This fool looked at his chest, then rushed me. "Aaaahhhhh, I kill you!" he roared.

Before I could get another shot off, he was all over me. His blood was pouring out on me. He bled all over me as I struggled to fight him off. He rammed into me again. I head butted him. He head butted me back instantly. This dude was an animal, and I was dizzy. I wasn't even the one with the gunshot wounds bleeding to death either. From my collar, I heard Laylow saying, "Shit, we got company." Then multiple gunshots rang out. I had to end this fight. Something was wrong. I pressed my fingers into his bullet wounds.

"Aaaahhhhh, Aaaahhhhh!" he screamed in agony as I drove him up against the closet. I kicked him in the nuts. Once he grabbed them off instinct, I put two in his head. *PFF, PFF!*

"Now get up from that," I said as he crashed through the closet. When he fell through the door, he fell on top of a black tarp. There was a pile of something underneath it. As his body slid down, there it was. Han Che's coke stacked high in a pile under the dead Russian. How did I know? It had a stamp on it of a red umbrella with a Chinese inscription over the umbrella. I'd learned the inscriptions meant "The Hands of Many." I guess because it went through so many different hands. I had no time because Laylow was in trouble and Polo had I guessed, took five once he kicked the bathroom door in. As I ran out of the room, I was met with a board to the face. Then there was nothing I could do because I was greeted by darkness.

How much time had passed? I didn't know. I was regaining consciousness. But I was zip tied with my hands behind me. I was in the living room, and I just knew I was dead. My head was pounding. I heard Polo talking shit, but he sounded hurt.

"Fuck you! Fuck you! Should have never fucking trusted you. I'll see you in hell," Polo spat, blood drooling from his mouth.

"Ah, good. He is awake. Now you can witness how this is done," Nikoli, the Russian I shot in the ass, said.

"Yay, fucking Han is…" before he could finish, Nikoli put two in his head with Polo's own gun. *PFF, PFF*!

My head hurt so bad! I could not even scream. Zip tied behind my back, laying on my side, just waiting for my turn. What the fuck went wrong? We had the drop, but we were ambushed somehow. Maybe Amanda "Good Pussy" Sanders set us up. But that thought vanished when she was brought into the living room kicking and screaming.

Two more men, I realized, were in the room. They brought her into the room naked, despite her desperate attempts to free herself from their grasp. They had raped and beaten her badly. The two men threw her in the middle of the floor like a ragdoll. Nikoli had the floor as the two men stepped back.

"So, bitch, you set me up, huh? Yes, you did, for these niggers." He walked up to her and kicked her in the face. "I can taste your fear, slut. You like to suck on shit, huh, tramp? Open up. Open your fucking mouth," he commanded, crazed.

When she refused to open her mouth, he rammed the gun inside. The force broke her front teeth. She let out an agonizing moan.

Nikoli looked at me. This show was for me. "Shhh, Shhhh. You sent them. Yes, you did." *PFF, PFF* "Now suck on that Amanda "Good Pussy" Sanders. Hmph, the pussy wasn't that good." They all laughed.

Another man was coming from upstairs saying something in Russian I couldn't understand. He was carrying a jug of gasoline with him. He poured it everywhere. He even poured some on Amanda, Laylow, and Polo. He said something in Russian to Nikoli. Then he looked at me. He seemed irritated. Then he said something in Russian as the other two men snatched me up and dragged me out of the house. I was thrown into a van. The keys were in the van already, and the guy with the jug of gasoline jumped inside the van behind the wheel. Nikoli came out with something in his hand. It was my damn grenade!

Speaking Russian with an English drawl, he said, "For a monkey, you have great taste in toys." He then took the pin off the grenade and threw it in the beach house. He jumped into the can, and as we took off there was a deafening explosion. The beach house was now a memory, along with every person and everything inside of it.

Nikoli had a needle in his hand, and he shot some liquid out of it. "As for you, my gold-toothed friend, it's nap time," he said as he stabbed the needle into my neck. As I drifted off, I wondered why I wasn't dead with the others. Why would he keep me alive? Were the drugs taken out of the closet from underneath their dead comrade before they blew up the house? As the van moved away from the explosion, and the sounds of emergency vehicles grew closer and closer, I slowly faded out. I hoped and prayed death would come quickly.

Chapter 16

Rude Awakening...

I was in the darkness, and I kept hearing the voice. "Your friend is also your enemy." I knew the voice now.

"Mom! Mom, I hear you, but I can't see you!"

"Be strong son, be strong. Not too much longer now."

Suddenly, there was a light over me, like a moon in the darkness. Rain poured down. I felt myself getting drenched somehow. My eyes were fluttering open. The light hurt so damn bad. Felt like my damn eyes were bleeding. I knew there was a knot on my forehead. Then a wave of cold water hit me. As I blinked away the water from my eyes, I looked at my clothes and realized they must have already thrown three buckets on me, trying to bring me back to wake me.

I looked around. I was in some kind of warehouse. Some windows were spray painted black, but not the windows up high. Three guys were playing cards at a table, and I could see the van was a little further back. Nikoli was smoking a cigarette as he put down, what I assumed was, the fourth bucket meant to wake me.

"Sleeping beauty, welcome back," he said, thumping the cigarette at me.

I promised myself if there was a God, and he allowed me, Nikoli was mine!

"Look at the way he looks at me. Why the hell are you keeping him alive?" Nikoli said. I thought he was talking to himself, until I heard a familiar voice that chilled me to my bones. He was walking down some steps, then towards me, and then he stopped right in front of me. This was a nightmare! It had to be a bad dream.

"Because, you idiot, he is my friend," Han said as he stood in front of me.

He was dressed in an all-gray Saint Laurent suit, all-black Saint Laurent loafers, and an all-black button up under the suit. *This some Machiavellian shit!* Han was still alive. WTH... I was so mind fucked that I just kept motionless except for blinking and trembling. He walked toward me with two pills and a bottle of water. He came near me and I jumped when he tried to give me the pills.

"Look Yay, if I wanted you dead, you would be dead. This will help with the headache. Nikoli only gave you a small dose of serum. It knocks you out, but a few milligrams more will have you like a corpse. Light pulse, but you still live. I'll explain everything to you. So, please, take the fucking pills," Han said with his cocky smile. For the first time I realized he did look like Jet Li, which was what Polo called him.

I opened my mouth, he popped the pills in, then poured water in my mouth. He went to the table where the three guys were playing cards, and he grabbed an extra chair. He nodded at Nikoli, and Nikoli gave me a look before walking to the table to join the others. I realized now that I was zip tied in the front and not the back. I looked over to where they were playing cards and realized the transmitter box to the receiver was on the table. Maybe they took it trying to figure out what it was before they blew the place up.

Han sat down the chair in front of me as he said, "Yay, I am so sorry you got caught up in this shit. I was actually hoping you would leave town. Damn it, Yayo, why didn't you just leave?" He ran his fingers through his slicked back hair.

"Han, what the fuck are you talking about? Why the hell would I leave town when they killed you?" Then I looked at him. "Well, I thought they killed you. If I'm your fucking friend, then why do you have me like a hostage in here?"

Han just shook his head. "Damn, Yay. You almost pulled it off. You even paid my old man half a million. When I told you to plan ahead, you listened. You have been a busy boy," Han said, wagging his finger at me.

"Han, you truly pissing me off. I got fucking shot thinking you were dead, and I could have died, tied up in whatever scheme you on," I said, realizing the pills did clear my head from a roar to a dull sort of ache.

"Now that, you can blame on Polo. After Nikoli stuck the serum in me, he shot the vest I had on. When you dapped me up and asked me had I gained weight, I thought you felt it. Crazy as this is, I fucking told Polo my scheme. I was taking over my father's business, that we were going to get robbed that night, and that once I took over, you two would be set for life. Why he even came with you is beyond me," he said, speaking Russian to one of the goons who brought over a bottle of vodka and two plastic cups.

"So, you speak Russian now? What is that shit all about?" I said, still confused and trying to catch up.

He poured us both some vodka. He tilted my cup to my lips. I drank it down, inviting the sting of the liquor in the back of my throat. He then took a drink from his own cup.

"Those Russians know how to make some good vodka," Han said, downing his whole cup. Then he said, "Yay, I actually speak several languages. What's this shit all about you ask?" Han then looked at me the way Han Che had in the Maybach, with the eyes of a killer, and continued, "You see, revenge is mine, Yay. That is what this is about. My piece of shit father got my mom killed. He could have saved her, but he let the Triads kill her. Now it's his turn. Simple as that," he said grinning menacingly, almost looking insanely mad.

"Triad? Aren't they Chinese too?" I spoke.

"That's why I always liked you, Yay. Yes, they are, but no. We are part of the same cartel, but not the Triad. When we were in California, they wanted goods shipped through the same pipeline my father had access to," Han said. taking a swig straight from the bottle now. "The man that killed my mother was named He, which means river. He was in love with my mom, but she was in love with my father. As time went on, both He and my father rose to power. He was a hothead though, killing everything if the means were available.

"He was selling heroin, boy, dog food, whatever you want to call it. Boatloads of it too." Han said something in Russian and then pulled out a cigarette. Nikoli came over and pulled out his lighter. When he gave Han a light, the flame came out high as hell.

"What the fuck, Nikoli? You got a damn flame thrower," Han said irritated. The other three men at the table snickered. Nikoli looked back at them with death in his eyes, as he pocketed the lighter.

"Sorry boss, but these assholes are playing pranks. Look, I know this is your friend, but he had a fucking picture of me on him. He will not join us," Nikoli said, walking back to the table and cursing at the men in Russian for making a fool of him in front of Han.

"What does hammer head mean by join us?" I asked Han.

"We will get to that part. Anyway, so my father refused He access to the pipeline, and this denial was seen as disrespect. War breaks out. He vanishes, but not before my mom had been killed," Han said, puffing out smoke. "So, we leave Compton, and we come here to set up shop. All the beaches were perfect. My father was a smart man, but he needed a supplier. These were the Russians. Now they had issues before, but money makes people forget certain things. A big shipment came in, which was one million grams," Han said.

"A fucking ton of coke? Damn, Han Che got it like that?" I said, having no idea how much a ton of coke would even cost. A million grams... That is a lot of coke!

"That's right. I forgot how damn good at math you are. Yes, a million grams is a ton. But imagine half of it gone to a Russian outfit that you already had issues with," Han said.

"But that would start a war, Han," I said, still not getting the picture.

"Of course it would, and the icing on the cake is your son. That would be me as a dead man, and then once the smoke clears..." Han said.

"You emerge and take over. And I'm guessing these flunkies," I said, nodding to the kats at the card table. "Will smooth things out with the Russians, which will give you power over the cartel and no hard feelings with the connect," I said.

Han stood up and clapped his hands together saying, "Very damn good, Yay. Shit, it sounds better when you say it. Once they smoke my pops, which according to my new comrades over there, is already in motion by a Mr. Diplo. You see, Mr. Diplo is their underboss, and he is after my father's head. Thanks to you, Danny and James, the two dudes you all killed, it's going to look like retaliation. I know my father. He is paranoid, and I know you too," Han said.

"Hell you mean by that? I thought I knew you. All this bullshit is between you and your father. Fuck you drag me in it for?" I said heated.

127

"I know if you had suspected something was up… However, when you learned the Russians robbed us that night, you went to my father and told him. He always liked you, Yay. He would never have killed you," Han said knowingly.

"But he had me scraping up one-point-five mil because of your dumbass. You lied in that text, and you put a hundred bricks in my hands. You piece of shit! You set me up!" I said, the zip ties stretching so hard across my skin, I felt the heat of my blood on my skin as it began to drip. I was angry and wanted my hands free so I could get them on Han for all this shit.

"Your friend is your enemy." I could still hear my mom's voice in my head. She was warning me even from the grave. "Be strong, son, be strong. It won't be much longer now." Did that mean I was getting ready to die? I was still alive for a reason. I knew Han, and he had some sick plan for me. I had to be cool and find the right angle.

"Sticks and stones, Yay. Look, Polo really set you up. I gave that bastard the location at the beach house, but the sad part is, he thought I was dead for real. It's a little funny actually. We couldn't get along, but he shot at my men thinking I was in danger," Han said. "How ironic is that?"

"Polo was your friend, Han," I said.

"No, fuck that. Polo was your friend. You know since we were kids, he picked on me. He was pissed that you and me were close friends. Fuck Polo. Stupid ass. He tried to rob the beach house because he knew the bricks were there," Han said.

"What?" I said confused.

"He played you, Yay. Listen, I don't know Laylow like that, but what did he tell you? I mean, he had to make some bullshit up like he just found out where they were," Han said to me.

I thought of the conversation. He had told me Laylow had said one of them sounded like one of the Russians off the movie *Rocky*.

"Motherfucka," I said out loud. Polo somehow got Laylow to claim he got a tip. Polo knew I was ready to ride for Han. Plus, we could have died. I thought Han was dead. He knew some of the scheme, but Han faking his death he had knowledge of. It had cost both Laylow and Polo their lives. Amanda just happened to be connected to Laylow, and it made it even more convincing for me. Damn! Nothing but lies. I had to get myself out of this mess. All this was because Han wanted his father dead. So, if he beefed with the Russians, once they smoke cleared, Han would be crowned.

"Damn, do I have anyone that didn't betray me?" I said with my head hung down.

"Yay, I know this all sounds really fucked up, but listen. I've scattered work around. My dad will not recover from half of the shipment gone. Once he is gone, as Jet Li once said, 'I'm the one.'" He laughed hysterically "Get it? I'm the one." He still chuckled at his own joke. He stepped on the cigarette, crushing it out with his foot, and then he sat back down.

"I was only trying to do this to avenge my mother. Come on Yay. You know how it is. You lost your mom as well," Han said.

"Don't you dare bring my mom into this game of chess with you and Han Che. Han, I could have died, man," I said.

"Look, I was already out of it when Nikoli hit me with the serum. They only shot back because they were fired upon. If Polo never came with you, everything would have went smooth. I never wanted anything to happen to you, but the way shit was going, you would have paid my father off.

That would have ruined my plans. I needed the tension between my father and the Russians to continue. There is, or was, a deadline for the shipment to be paid off."

Han leaned forward in his chair and stared at me. "I'm the man now, Yay. I have the Russians infiltrated. Money will forever compromise loyalty. Yay, will you join me?" Han said, hands on his knees, staring at me. I had to play this right because Han was so sick with revenge on his father, he refused to see how he had put my life in danger. The transmitter on the table had a green light that lit up. No one noticed it except me. I kept Han talking.

"What is in it for me, Han? A hot bath and a change of clothes at least? I'm zip tied and sitting on the hard ass floor drenched in water. Plus, my best friend has miraculously returned from the dead. So, tell me, what is in it for me?" I said, hiding my anger from Han.

Han smiled at me.

"I'm glad you asked that question. Did you ever wonder to yourself how I got the drop on you at the beach house? You have to understand I had to stay in hiding. But I had someone who I, unfortunately, told my secret to," Han said staring at me.

"Told your secret to who, Han?" I asked. "You still got me breathing, so what's in it for me. You telling me that you exposed the fact that you are still alive to someone else? I don't think it was Polo, he gone, and you didn't even know Laylow." I was thinking, *could it be Patron?* But that wouldn't make sense. Han said something to one of the Russians at the table. One of the guys that had put me in the van stood and went up the same stairs Han had come down from. When he came back down the stairs, he had a hostage. *Just when I had thought things could not get any worse.* One of the Russians brought Milk Marie in front of me, bound and gagged. Her makeup was smeared from crying. He sat her down in the chair Han had been sitting in and walked back over to the table.

Nikoli was grinning at me. As bad as I wanted to wipe that grin off of his face, I was busy trying to steal glances at the transmitter box for the blinking green light. I looked at Milk Marie, and she looked like she was scared to death. I kept my poker face on, giving away nothing. I wanted to live.

"Okay. You got Milk Marie. So what? Fuck that got to do with me? She don't got nothing to do with this, Han." I said, trying not to look at Milk Marie. "What's up, man?"

"What's up?" he repeated, pushing her head violently. "This bitch, that's what's up. Some weeks ago, you two had an argument. I was in Thumpers in Elizabeth City, having some drinks. She strolls in looking mad as hell. She ordered two blue motorcycles and drinks one down. Then she sips the other one. I speak to her, and the next thing you know, we playing pool. She just kept bending that ass over to take shots, going on about just wanting to have fun, why did things have to be complicated... My Lamborghini Aventador was outside," Han said, looked at Milk Marie like she was fucking Kim Kardashian or something.

"She said she had never driven a Lamborghini before." Han looked at me and smiled. "Imagine that, but I know you girls love when you flash. I fucked her all night, and she realized some Chinese men don't have little dicks."

Milk Marie was trying to say something through her gag that sounded a lot like, "Fuck you."

"Been there and done that," Han said. "Now I know why they call this bitch 'Milk Marie.' My, my, my, the bitch sucked me dry." Han taunted me, trying to see my reaction. I was boiling inside. The betrayal by so many so damn quickly was dizzying, but I put my game face on.

"Okay. You fucked and got sucked by Milk Marie. Fuck you two humping got to do with me?" I said nonchalantly. He seemed to be buying my bullshit.

"Yeah, Yay, you a true playa. I knew you would understand. Anyway, she gets up the next day feeling guilty. At least, that was what she told me. I heard her begging her mom and asking if she could crash with her for a few days. I never saw her again, until tonight that is," he said, rubbing her face gently. If I was reading his actions correctly, I would have sworn he was gone over Milk Marie.

"Anyway, I called her up. I told her I had faked my death to hide from whoever did the robbery, until I found the people responsible." He looked over at me speaking matter of factly. "I mean shit, I am supposed to be dead. You see all the trouble they caused," he said, nodding at the men at the table, "trying to get some pussy. That Amanda chic almost got them whacked. I was horny. Anyway, she claims she sorry, but she couldn't come to me. The bitch said she had to tell you. She said he loved you and hung up on me."

"Okay. You were trying to bust a nut with someone you knew to stay low key. Big deal," I said, glancing at the transmitter box, which was now glowing a steady green.

"I had her followed, and my boys caught her coming out of some apartment. Anyway, she was brought back here, but only after we followed you to Corolla. Make sense now?" Han said, rubbing Milk Marie's hair.

"Yeah. It makes sense. Everyone I know is a fucking liar," I said, while staring hard at Milk Marie.

"Ouch, wait a minute. I'm spilling out everything to you. I didn't lie to you. You just had no knowledge of what I was up to. You asked me what you had to do, right?" Han looked at the men at the table. All of them came over and huddled around.

"Yeah, I did," I said irritated. Han pulled out a blade and cut my zip ties. I rubbed my wrists. Han took out a Colt 45, cocked the gun, took the clip out, and handed me the gun with one in the head. Nikoli, not liking that I now had a weapon, took his gun out. Han was standing on the other side of Milk Marie. As I took the gun from Han's hand, he politely said, "Shoot her, and you are in with us. It is not such a difficult task being that she is a disloyal little trollop."

"Yo, Yay, if you hear me nod your head." It was Patron. I could hear him on the receiver still attached to my collar. I nodded my head up and down. Han thought I was agreeing to shoot Milk Marie. I raised the gun to Milk Marie. Tears flowed off her face.

"Good. Now it's about to get ugly. Just do me a favor. Step to the right just a little bit homie." I did as I was told, and I stepped to the right. Then I heard four shots whizz by me. *Boom, Boom, Boom, Boom*! Three of the Russians dropped, all head shots, and there was brain matter everywhere. Nikoli only got grazed. Damn! Han took off running. I shot him in the leg.

"Ah fuck!" he shouted in pain, stumbled, but still running but with a limp now. Nikoli recovered, but since my gun had no more bullets, I threw it at him and charged him like a linebacker with all the energy I had left inside me. I fell to the floor with all of my weight on him. I felt a sharp pain in my side. Nikoli had stabbed me. We were face-to-face, rolling on the floor, Nikoli managed to keep his hand on the knife, which was still stuck in my side. Nikoli was getting up looking dazed. I threw vodka all over him like it was Holy water, and I was doing an exorcism on his ass.

"Burn in hell, you piece of shit!" I then took a mouth full of vodka, lit the lighter with the flame as high as a torch, and I spit the vodka right into the single flame. It hit Nikoli in his face, dead center, with a huge *WHOOSH*.

"Ah, ah, ah!" Nikoli screamed out in agony. The door to the warehouse exploded. Then Wang walked through the smoke shooting and filling Nikoli's body, already engulfed in flames, with bullets. *Boom, Boom, Boom!* Nikoli dropped to the floor. The smell of his burning flesh was unbearable. Han was fast limping to the back of the warehouse when *BOOM*, it exploded too.

Fujj walked through the rubble and smoke with a 40-caliber cannon aimed right at Han. Han dropped to his knees and began laughing hysterically as he screamed at Fujj manically, "Kill me! Just do it! Ha, ha, ha, do it! Do it! Kill me!"

Fujj just stared at Han in complete and total disgust, not impressed with his pathetic show. Wang was untying Milk Marie, and he was speaking into a radio. He said, "All clear, Mr. Han Che."

Then, through the debris and haze of smoke, Han Che walked in wearing a Balenciaga suit. He had on brown gators and a matching brown tie. He had a brown suit coat draped over his shoulders. A fedora hat with a black feather tipped just over his eyes. He looked around and shook his head. He nodded to the van. Wang started loading up the bricks, and just about that time, two more Russian guys came in with guns drawn.

"Han Che, look out!" I yelled from the floor, still holding onto my bloody side. Han Che didn't even flinch.

"No worries. They are with us. It took some time but we, meaning Mr. Diplo and myself, got to the bottom of things." Han Che said, flicking imaginary lint off his expensive suit.

Fujj dragged Han to the chair Milk Marie was sitting in. She came to stand by my side, but I waved her away.

"See, two hundred bricks didn't show in Kentucky. Mr. Diplo, just like me, is a very paranoid man. Several drops were not going where they were supposed to. Nikoli," he nodded toward the now smoking and stinking corpse on the floor, "had loose lips. Complaining about his position. Therefore, we followed up on him," Han Che said.

"How did you even know I was here?" I said, holding my side and feeling exhausted.

Han Che pulled out what looked like a GPS tracker. He waved it around me, dug in my Dickies pocket, and pulled out my phone. The GPS device started to beep rapidly.

"You been tracking me this whole time. You knew my moves before I even made them," I said, out of breath but glad to be breathing still.

"Well, of course. Virginia Beach, Moyock, Elizabeth City and Edenton, etc. However, thanks to Patron, we got a line on you when you came here," Han Che said and on cue, Patron strolled into the warehouse with the sniper rifle on his shoulder.

"What's up, big brother? I told you I was coming," he said grinning. He came over to my side and helped me up. I almost fell back down, so he walked me over to the chair I was originally sitting in.

"Fool, I thought you were in Richmond flipping that gas," I said, taking the cloth they had Milk Marie tied up with and stuffing my wound with it. Then I tied another long piece around my waist. God, it hurt bad. The pain was searing through my side, but I needed to hear how my ass just got rescued.

"Well, you know the job we did on the strip? Well, I love this 007 shit. I never gave back the receiver. So, for the hell of it, I brought it. I could see through the top windows with my scope. I got up with Han Che, and I told him you were avenging Han. I told him you were going at some Russians. All of us got here after Han Che picked up your phone signal. I would have popped them fools at the table, but," he stared at Han, "seeing Han alive had me fucked up. But, hey, I got three out of four. Right?"

"Yeah, the dumb asses brought the transmitter box with them. When it glowed green, I knew another receiver had to be around. I wasn't expecting you to be the one with the receiver though." We both dapped.

"Anytime, fam, but you need stitches pronto," Patron said.

I then looked at Milk Marie. She was just standing there shaking. I got up, found the Colt 45 beside Nikoli's charred body and went to Han. Han leaned up and looked at me. I punched the shit out of him. I knocked him right out of the chair. Blood sprayed from his face. Neither Han Che, Wang, nor Fujj moved an inch to help him. I dug in his pocket and found the clip to the gun. I slammed the clip into the gun, and I walked over to Milk Marie.

"Whoa. Whoa. Yay, man. Be cool. Wait a minute," Patron said.

"No. Fuck that wait shit. I took care of this bitch, and she got Polo and Laylow killed."

"Damn, man. Look. I have to tell you something," Patron said, standing beside me as I had the gun raised and pointed at Milk's face. "She the one told me Han was alive. When she called me again, I told her you weren't with me. I was on the highway then. She said you had went out looking for Han's killers, but Han wasn't dead. Also, she is pregnant, Yay," Patron said.

"Pregnant? Shit... By who? Han? Man, I am fucking outta here," I said, still aiming the gun at Milk. Pointing it straight in her disloyal, lying, fucking face.

"It's yours, homie, and I believe her. She told me everything. I know it's fucked up, but if you kill her then you will also be killing your seed," Patron said his hands on my shoulders. "It's all over. We good, big bruh."

I lowered the gun from Milk Marie's face, and then spit right in the middle of it. I told her, "If that baby not mine, I'm slumping you. We done though, and that's a fact."

She wiped her face. She was still crying. She nodded at me. I was beyond pissed. All this betrayal was too much. Now all eyes were on Han.

"All of you need to leave now. My son and I need to talk. There is a black Denali with the hundred bricks in it." Han Che looked at me. "It's yours. I am sorry for the confusion. Now leave us," Han Che said.

Patron helped me up, and Milk Marie was walking out. I looked back at Han one last time. My friend, my boy... All of this over a grudge against his own father. I shook my head and limped out with Patron. Two of the Russians with Han Che were posted up outside. One of them had the keys to Milk Marie's Tahoe. After checking the pockets of all the bodies, they nodded at Patron and me. We got in the truck and drove past Milk Marie, who was standing next to the Tahoe crying.

"I know you feel some type of way, but she got me to convince Han Che to be on you tonight. Shit, when she told me Han was alive, I almost didn't believe her. Shit, what we going to do now?" Patron said.

I leaned back into the passenger seat. I watched the image of Milk Marie fading away in the rearview mirror. "I don't know, but like Jay-Z said, 'I got 99 problems but a bitch ain't one,'" I said grinning.

"Nigga, you got a hundred bricks. You already know what it is," Patron said, putting more distance between us and the gruesome murder scene.

"Yeah, broke niggas make noise," I said.

"But rich niggas make moves," Patron said. "Yo, I got this chic. She a nurse. She can stitch you right up. I got you, my gee."

"I got you too, bruh."

We dapped up and kept it pushing.

Meanwhile...

"My own damn flesh and blood. Why, Han? Why go through all this trouble? Your mother's death was not my fault. It was He Sun who killed my Charlotte."

"It was you, Pop!" Han spat the words at his father in rage, spittle spraying from his mouth like venom. "They killed Mom because you wouldn't share the pipeline. I hold you responsible."

Han Che shook his head. "If I would have let He smuggle anything through my pipeline, the Triads would have eventually moved on the Cartel. Then my foolish son, your mother, you, and I would have been a memory." Han Che looked at Fujj, who handed him the 40-caliber cannon gun. He took the gun from Fujj and looking at his son in the eyes, Han Che said, "This is why I didn't want you in this life, Han. Now you must pay for the consequences of your actions." Han Che raised the 40-caliber to Han's face.

One of the Russians said from the doorway, "Hey, Han Che, we need to get out of here. The scanner is reporting there are units headed this way."

Han Che turned his head and responded, "Okay. Almost done."

Han jumped out of the chair and pushed Han Che. Then he dove out a window. Glass was breaking as Wang and Han Che unloaded their weapons in Han's direction. They ran outside to find out Han must have cleared the window and went straight into the freezing river waters.

"Either he will die of hypothermia or the gators will get him, but we have to go, boss," Wang said. Han Che stared out at the dark, choppy waters. It was cold and death was all over the warehouse.

Two Russian men had put C-4 in the warehouse in different areas. They all left, and then when they were a safe distance away, set off the charges using a remote detonator.

KABOOM

Like Fourth of July fireworks, the sky lit up from the explosion. Wang and Fujj were making their escape in the Maybach. Wang was driving, with Fujj in the passenger seat. Han Che was in the back, pouring himself some Louis XIII. He took a deep, cleansing breath.

The Russians were still on his side, and they made up for the loss of work. Mr. Diplo and Han Che were still in good standing. As Han Che sipped his expensive liquor, he thought, *it's finally over…*

Fre$h

Chapter 17

The Good, The Bad, The Ugly...

One Year Later

I was on the beach, still thinking of how far we had come. I had moved in with Shavonda, who was devastated about Laylow's death. She didn't blame me though. We had a big gathering at the Waterfront for Laylow and Polo. I gave Tawana and now nine-year-old Crystal two hundred thousand dollars. I never let her know it came from me, but I am sure she had her suspicions. I found Laylow's parents and gave them the same.

I had spoken to Milk Marie three months ago, and she had a baby boy. He was mine. I named him Malcolm after Malcolm X. Malcolm Seemiyun Baxter Jr. My son was handsome, and for a time I wondered if things had been different, how it would have been. Milk Marie refused to take the cook house apartment. I had moved everything out at the duplex. I kept it furnished though for when I was in town. I was the owner of a business coined 5-Tint. I had them spread out all over Virginia.

I still had a third share ownership at the duplex, and I sold both of my first two tiny window businesses. Pedro got one, and we just shook hands to seal the deal. Pedro was well trusted. His body shop was very lucrative.

Patron was still with this dark-skinned chic named Lisa. She was the nurse who sewed up my wound. She was pretty. She reminded me of Maxine from the show, *Living Single*. The equipment I had sparked an interest in Patron. He opened up a hunting shop with rifles, duck calling equipment, and other random wares for hunting.

I was happy for him, and I was glad we were out of the streets. Don't get me wrong. Han Che kept that work coming, and I promised myself just one more year, then I was out for good. Even though things were bad at one point, they were starting to look good again.

Milk Marie was working at a Popeyes restaurant on the beach. Shavonda had taken me out to eat there. She had her own apartment, and I think her kids would come over from time to time. Milk Marie even said to me once, jokingly, that her mom had even stayed a little while to visit. She made the comment when I had showed up at her job in order to show her the paternity test results, which had been sent straight to me via the mail.

Her manager was a light-skinned guy that acted real white. He just eyed us. I suspected they were dating, but that was none of my business. As long as my son was good, then I was good. Milk Marie and me never discussed or made mention of that night. I can tell she regretted it. It didn't matter. I was happy with Shavonda.

She was walking toward me out of the water, in her Givenchy bathing suit.. Damn, she was fine! Her hair was dyed blonde. She had it slicked back in a ponytail, looking like Amber Rose. Damn. Now I knew why Kanye West made the *Heartbreak* album. My boo had booty for days. Shit, even the women on the beach were looking.

I was in my beach chair underneath a big umbrella with no shirt on. My dreads were in a ponytail down my back, Calvin Klein shorts, Calvin Klein flip flops, and the necklace with my mom's picture was laying on my stomach. I was sipping on Grey Goose with a touch of pineapple juice. It was in a mug with a straw that claimed, "Virginia is for lovers."

"Whew. That was a nice swim. It feels good out there," Shavonda said, toweling herself off.

"Feels like life to me, and I'm truly enjoying it with you," I said, sipping my drink through the straw. She reached over and rubbed the scar on my right shoulder.

"I'm glad, baby. The past is the past. I'm pleased I'm off today. I need to hire someone," she said, sipping orange juice with a straw from her matching mug.

"Hey, it's not my fault. I tried and you said you got it," I said to her. I realized she was good at selling goods, so I helped her open a sporting goods store right on the strip. It was doing well, and it was tourist season. Don't get me wrong, Shavonda had her own money, but I had to admit I was falling for her. I couldn't tell her I loved her yet. The issue with Milk Marie and Han had left a bad taste in my mouth that had not faded yet. However, I felt I could trust Shavonda, and she was gorgeous. That was good enough for now.

"Well, I'm putting a help wanted sign up tomorrow. I definitely don't miss the DMV," she said, rubbing her feet in the sand.

We packed up and went home. I loved the way Shavonda was. She was a neat freak like me. We had a sunroom where we both undressed. On the patio, we had a shower where we could stand and wash the sand off. Then we would run inside the house together, naked, and we would take a real shower together. She said she learned her lesson when her bathtub kept clogging up with sand. Shavonda had the sunroom built right before I moved in. I had even taken Shavonda to meet my aunt, which I had never done with Milk Marie.

"My my, my... Nephew, if you brought her all the way to Woodbridge to see me, then she must be a keeper." Aunt Nancy laughed. That was six months ago.

After a shower and sex on top of the marble countertop in the kitchen, we were chilling together in the living room. It was late now, a little past midnight. We were watching *The Godfather*. You know the one where Al Pacino is old, and they try to put a hit on him in a family meeting. Anyway, Shavonda was dozing off, leaning on my shoulder. I put the blunt of Purple Haze out, which I had gotten from Patron. That was Patron's hustle though, loud. I am a coke boy. It's as simple as that.

The gangsters rushed Al Pacino out of the room to protect him on the TV as my phone started to ring. It dawned on me that I had never gotten rid of the phone Han Che had given me. A year had flown by, and I never thought about it until this moment. The ringtone played Gucci Mane's, "I don't mess with them unless they got an M, unless they got them M's."

"Yeah, this Yay," I answered.

"Yay, we need to talk. It's very important." Wang said.

Shavonda got up, yawned, and kissed me. Then she sashayed to the kitchen. When she cut the light on, she screamed. I jumped up, thinking she saw either a bug or a mouse. Shavonda was terrified of bugs.

"Yo, Wang, what the fuck! How did you get in here?" I said, trying to calm Shavonda down.

"Jesus, you know them?" Shavonda asked, her eyes still wide. Their size must have terrified her. She never asked me much about all that had happened. She was even understanding about Milk Marie being pregnant. But explaining my best friend had set me up to get back at his father, who was part of the Chinese Cartel, was just too much. To be connected like that for a young black guy was rare.

"Fujj picked the lock," Wang said.

Fujj grunted in agreement. The grunt also seemed to carry an apology. Fujj never spoke. Wang never took off his shades. Not in any of the time since I had met either of them. "I'm sorry, Yayo Sun, but it is urgent. Han Che is dead."

To Be Continued...
Betrayal of a Thug 2
Coming Soon

Acknowledgement

First of all, I thank God for being by my side and blessing me with a talent that has helped me hold on to my sanity. To my son, Malik Barnes, I wish I could hear from you. Good luck on your movies. One love to my fam Kwame Teague. I remember trying to hang back in the Rollingwood Dayz. One love to Goldsboro, Webbtown stand up. To those passed on that I miss dearly. To my mother, Shirley Ann Dunn, every day I know you are looking down, helping me. To Odell "Ozzy" Thomas, Temarcus "T-Bone" Thomas, Greg Speed, Royce Faircloth, Shawn Best, Marquell Honeycut, and RIP to Shelley T Lamb. Thank you, Allison Lamb, for the flicks in the beginning. To my loving best friend, Stacie Noelle Strickland, and my daughter, Alma Strickland for always being by my side when no one else was. Thank you both for your unconditional love that will be rewarded a hundred-fold. For those I didn't name, in the words of my dude Jay-Z, "You didn't remember me, so I don't remember you." Song Cry - Amen!

About the Author

FRE$H, Samuel Geddie, is from the rough streets of Webbtown Goldsboro, NC, USA. FRE$H is also the author of several other novels including:

Betrayal of a Thug Vol. I
Betrayal of a Thug Vol. II: The Search for Han
Do What I Got To Do.
Expect more soon and view his writing on Amazon

Fre$h

Lock Down Publications and Ca$h Presents assisted
publishing packages.

BASIC PACKAGE $499

Editing

Cover Design

Formatting

UPGRADED PACKAGE $800

Typing

Editing

Cover Design

Formatting

ADVANCE PACKAGE $1,200

Typing

Editing

Cover Design

Formatting

Copyright registration

Proofreading

Upload book to Amazon

LDP SUPREME PACKAGE $1,500

Typing

Editing

Cover Design

Formatting

Copyright registration

Proofreading

Set up Amazon account

Upload book to Amazon

Advertise on LDP Amazon and Facebook page

***Other services available upon request. Additional charges may apply

Lock Down Publications

P.O. Box 944

Stockbridge, GA 30281-9998

Phone # 470 303-9761

Submission Guideline

Submit the first three chapters of your completed manuscript to ldpsubmissions@gmail.com, subject line: Your book's title. The manuscript must be in a .doc file and sent as an attachment. Document should be in Times New Roman, double spaced and in size 12 font. Also, provide your synopsis and full contact information. If sending multiple submissions, they must each be in a separate email.

Have a story but no way to send it electronically? You can still submit to LDP/Ca$h Presents. Send in the first three chapters, written or typed, of your completed manuscript to:

LDP: Submissions Dept
Po Box 944
Stockbridge, Ga 30281

DO NOT send original manuscript. Must be a duplicate.

Provide your synopsis and a cover letter containing your full contact information.

Thanks for considering LDP and Ca$h Presents.

NEW RELEASES

SAVAGE STORMS 3 by MEESHA
LOYAL TO THE SOIL 3 by JIBRIL WILLIAMS
THE STREETS WILL NEVER CLOSE by K'AJJI
MONEY IN THE GRAVE 3 by MARTELL "TROUBLESOME"
BOLDEN
BETRAYAL OF A THUG by FRE$H

3X KRAZY III

STRAIGHT BEAST MODE II

De'Kari

KINGPIN KILLAZ IV

STREET KINGS III

PAID IN BLOOD III

CARTEL KILLAZ IV

DOPE GODS III

Hood Rich

SINS OF A HUSTLA II

ASAD

RICH $AVAGE II

By Martell Troublesome Bolden

YAYO V

Bred In The Game 2

S. Allen

CREAM III

By Yolanda Moore

SON OF A DOPE FIEND III

HEAVEN GOT A GHETTO II

By Renta

LOYALTY AIN'T PROMISED III

By Keith Williams

I'M NOTHING WITHOUT HIS LOVE II

SINS OF A THUG II

TO THE THUG I LOVED BEFORE II

IN A HUSTLER I TRUST II

Fre$h

By **Monet Dragun**
QUIET MONEY IV
EXTENDED CLIP III
THUG LIFE IV
By **Trai'Quan**
THE STREETS MADE ME IV
By **Larry D. Wright**
IF YOU CROSS ME ONCE II
By **Anthony Fields**
THE STREETS WILL NEVER CLOSE III
By **K'ajji**
HARD AND RUTHLESS III
THE BILLIONAIRE BENTLEYS III
Von Diesel
KILLA KOUNTY III
By **Khufu**
MONEY GAME III
By **Smoove Dolla**
JACK BOYS VS DOPE BOYS II
A GANGSTA'S QUR'AN V
By **Romell Tukes**
MURDA WAS THE CASE II
Elijah R. Freeman
THE STREETS NEVER LET GO II
By **Robert Baptiste**
AN UNFORESEEN LOVE III
By **Meesha**

KING OF THE TRENCHES III
by **GHOST & TRANAY ADAMS**

MONEY MAFIA II
LOYAL TO THE SOIL III
By **Jibril Williams**

QUEEN OF THE ZOO II
By **Black Migo**

THE BRICK MAN IV
THE COCAINE PRINCESS III
By King Rio

VICIOUS LOYALTY II
By Kingpen

A GANGSTA'S PAIN II
By J-Blunt

CONFESSIONS OF A JACKBOY III
By Nicholas Lock

GRIMEY WAYS II
By Ray Vinci

KING KILLA II
By Vincent "Vitto" Holloway

BETRAYAL OF A THUG II
By Fre$h

Available Now

RESTRAINING ORDER **I & II**
By **CA$H & Coffee**
LOVE KNOWS NO BOUNDARIES **I II & III**
By **Coffee**
RAISED AS A GOON I, II, III & IV
BRED BY THE SLUMS I, II, III
BLAST FOR ME I & II
ROTTEN TO THE CORE I II III
A BRONX TALE I, II, III
DUFFLE BAG CARTEL I II III IV V VI
HEARTLESS GOON I II III IV V
A SAVAGE DOPEBOY I II
DRUG LORDS I II III
CUTTHROAT MAFIA I II
KING OF THE TRENCHES
By **Ghost**
LAY IT DOWN **I & II**
LAST OF A DYING BREED I II
BLOOD STAINS OF A SHOTTA I & II III
By **Jamaica**
LOYAL TO THE GAME I II III
LIFE OF SIN I, II III
By **TJ & Jelissa**

BLOODY COMMAS I & II

SKI MASK CARTEL I II & III

KING OF NEW YORK I II,III IV V

RISE TO POWER I II III

COKE KINGS I II III IV V

BORN HEARTLESS I II III IV

KING OF THE TRAP I II

By **T.J. Edwards**

IF LOVING HIM IS WRONG…I & II

LOVE ME EVEN WHEN IT HURTS I II III

By **Jelissa**

WHEN THE STREETS CLAP BACK I & II III

THE HEART OF A SAVAGE I II III

MONEY MAFIA

LOYAL TO THE SOIL I II

By **Jibril Williams**

A DISTINGUISHED THUG STOLE MY HEART I II & III

LOVE SHOULDN'T HURT I II III IV

RENEGADE BOYS I II III IV

PAID IN KARMA I II III

SAVAGE STORMS I II III

AN UNFORESEEN LOVE I II

By **Meesha**

A GANGSTER'S CODE I &, II III

A GANGSTER'S SYN I II III

THE SAVAGE LIFE I II III

CHAINED TO THE STREETS I II III

BLOOD ON THE MONEY I II III

A GANGSTA'S PAIN

By J-Blunt

PUSH IT TO THE LIMIT

By **Bre' Hayes**

BLOOD OF A BOSS **I, II, III, IV, V**

SHADOWS OF THE GAME

TRAP BASTARD

By **Askari**

THE STREETS BLEED MURDER **I, II & III**

THE HEART OF A GANGSTA I II& III

By **Jerry Jackson**

CUM FOR ME I II III IV V VI VII VIII

An **LDP Erotica Collaboration**

BRIDE OF A HUSTLA **I II & II**

THE FETTI GIRLS **I, II& III**

CORRUPTED BY A GANGSTA I, II III, IV

BLINDED BY HIS LOVE

THE PRICE YOU PAY FOR LOVE I, II ,III

DOPE GIRL MAGIC I II III

By **Destiny Skai**

WHEN A GOOD GIRL GOES BAD

By **Adrienne**

THE COST OF LOYALTY I II III

By Kweli

A GANGSTER'S REVENGE **I II III & IV**

THE BOSS MAN'S DAUGHTERS I II III IV V

A SAVAGE LOVE **I & II**

BAE BELONGS TO ME I II

A HUSTLER'S DECEIT I, II, III

WHAT BAD BITCHES DO I, II, III

SOUL OF A MONSTER I II III

KILL ZONE

A DOPE BOY'S QUEEN I II III

By **Aryanna**

A KINGPIN'S AMBITON

A KINGPIN'S AMBITION **II**

I MURDER FOR THE DOUGH

By **Ambitious**

TRUE SAVAGE I II III IV V VI VII

DOPE BOY MAGIC I, II, III

MIDNIGHT CARTEL I II III

CITY OF KINGZ I II

NIGHTMARE ON SILENT AVE

THE PLUG OF LIL MEXICO II

By **Chris Green**

A DOPEBOY'S PRAYER

By **Eddie "Wolf" Lee**

THE KING CARTEL **I, II & III**

By **Frank Gresham**

THESE NIGGAS AIN'T LOYAL **I, II & III**

By **Nikki Tee**

GANGSTA SHYT **I II &III**

By **CATO**

THE ULTIMATE BETRAYAL

By **Phoenix**

BOSS'N UP **I , II & III**

By **Royal Nicole**

I LOVE YOU TO DEATH

By **Destiny J**

I RIDE FOR MY HITTA

I STILL RIDE FOR MY HITTA

By **Misty Holt**

LOVE & CHASIN' PAPER

By **Qay Crockett**

TO DIE IN VAIN

SINS OF A HUSTLA

By **ASAD**

BROOKLYN HUSTLAZ

By **Boogsy Morina**

BROOKLYN ON LOCK I & II

By **Sonovia**

GANGSTA CITY

By **Teddy Duke**

A DRUG KING AND HIS DIAMOND I & II III

A DOPEMAN'S RICHES

HER MAN, MINE'S TOO I, II

CASH MONEY HO'S

THE WIFEY I USED TO BE I II

By **Nicole Goosby**

TRAPHOUSE KING **I II & III**

KINGPIN KILLAZ I II III

STREET KINGS I II

PAID IN BLOOD **I II**

CARTEL KILLAZ I II III

DOPE GODS I II

By **Hood Rich**

LIPSTICK KILLAH **I, II, III**

CRIME OF PASSION I II & III

FRIEND OR FOE I II III

By **Mimi**

STEADY MOBBN' **I, II, III**

THE STREETS STAINED MY SOUL I II III

By **Marcellus Allen**

WHO SHOT YA **I, II, III**

SON OF A DOPE FIEND I II

HEAVEN GOT A GHETTO

Renta

GORILLAZ IN THE BAY **I II III IV**

TEARS OF A GANGSTA I II

3X KRAZY I II

STRAIGHT BEAST MODE

DE'KARI

TRIGGADALE I II III

MURDAROBER WAS THE CASE

Elijah R. Freeman

GOD BLESS THE TRAPPERS I, II, III

THESE SCANDALOUS STREETS I, II, III

FEAR MY GANGSTA I, II, III IV, V

THESE STREETS DON'T LOVE NOBODY I, II

BURY ME A G I, II, III, IV, V

A GANGSTA'S EMPIRE I, II, III, IV

THE DOPEMAN'S BODYGAURD I II

THE REALEST KILLAZ I II III

THE LAST OF THE OGS I II III

Tranay Adams

THE STREETS ARE CALLING

Duquie Wilson

MARRIED TO A BOSS I II III

By Destiny Skai & Chris Green

KINGZ OF THE GAME I II III IV V VI

Playa Ray

SLAUGHTER GANG I II III

RUTHLESS HEART I II III

By Willie Slaughter

FUK SHYT

By Blakk Diamond

DON'T F#CK WITH MY HEART I II

By Linnea

ADDICTED TO THE DRAMA I II III

IN THE ARM OF HIS BOSS II

By Jamila

YAYO I II III IV

A SHOOTER'S AMBITION I II

BRED IN THE GAME

By S. Allen

TRAP GOD I II III

RICH $AVAGE

MONEY IN THE GRAVE I II III

By Martell Troublesome Bolden

FOREVER GANGSTA

GLOCKS ON SATIN SHEETS I II

By Adrian Dulan

TOE TAGZ I II III IV

LEVELS TO THIS SHYT I II

By Ah'Million

KINGPIN DREAMS I II III

By Paper Boi Rari

CONFESSIONS OF A GANGSTA I II III IV

CONFESSIONS OF A JACKBOY I II

By Nicholas Lock

I'M NOTHING WITHOUT HIS LOVE

SINS OF A THUG

TO THE THUG I LOVED BEFORE

A GANGSTA SAVED XMAS

IN A HUSTLER I TRUST

By Monet Dragun

CAUGHT UP IN THE LIFE I II III

THE STREETS NEVER LET GO

By Robert Baptiste

NEW TO THE GAME I II III

MONEY, MURDER & MEMORIES I II III

By **Malik D. Rice**

LIFE OF A SAVAGE I II III

A GANGSTA'S QUR'AN I II III IV

MURDA SEASON I II III

GANGLAND CARTEL I II III

CHI'RAQ GANGSTAS I II III

KILLERS ON ELM STREET I II III

JACK BOYZ N DA BRONX I II III

A DOPEBOY'S DREAM I II III

JACK BOYS VS DOPE BOYS

By **Romell Tukes**

LOYALTY AIN'T PROMISED I II

By Keith Williams

QUIET MONEY I II III

THUG LIFE I II III

EXTENDED CLIP I II

By **Trai'Quan**

THE STREETS MADE ME I II III

By **Larry D. Wright**

THE ULTIMATE SACRIFICE I, II, III, IV, V, VI

KHADIFI

IF YOU CROSS ME ONCE

ANGEL I II

IN THE BLINK OF AN EYE

By **Anthony Fields**

THE LIFE OF A HOOD STAR

By Ca$h & Rashia Wilson
THE STREETS WILL NEVER CLOSE I II
By K'ajji
CREAM I II
By Yolanda Moore
NIGHTMARES OF A HUSTLA I II III
By King Dream
CONCRETE KILLA I II
VICIOUS LOYALTY
By Kingpen
HARD AND RUTHLESS I II
MOB TOWN 251
THE BILLIONAIRE BENTLEYS I II
By Von Diesel
GHOST MOB
Stilloan Robinson
MOB TIES I II III IV V
By SayNoMore
BODYMORE MURDERLAND I II III
By Delmont Player
FOR THE LOVE OF A BOSS
By C. D. Blue
MOBBED UP I II III IV
THE BRICK MAN I II III
THE COCAINE PRINCESS I II
By King Rio
KILLA KOUNTY I II

Fre$h

By Khufu

MONEY GAME I II

By Smoove Dolla

A GANGSTA'S KARMA I II

By FLAME

KING OF THE TRENCHES I II

by **GHOST & TRANAY ADAMS**

QUEEN OF THE ZOO

By **Black Migo**

GRIMEY WAYS

By Ray Vinci

XMAS WITH AN ATL SHOOTER

By Ca$h & Destiny Skai

KING KILLA

By Vincent "Vitto" Holloway

BETRAYAL OF A THUG

By Fre$h

<u>BOOKS BY LDP'S CEO, CA$H</u>

TRUST IN NO MAN

TRUST IN NO MAN 2

TRUST IN NO MAN 3

BONDED BY BLOOD

SHORTY GOT A THUG

THUGS CRY

THUGS CRY 2

THUGS CRY 3

TRUST NO BITCH

TRUST NO BITCH 2

TRUST NO BITCH 3

TIL MY CASKET DROPS

RESTRAINING ORDER

RESTRAINING ORDER 2

IN LOVE WITH A CONVICT

LIFE OF A HOOD STAR

XMAS WITH AN ATL SHOOTER

Fre$h